Alex

Li

Paulo

Hex

Amber

ALPHA FORCE

Also available in the *Alpha Force* series:

SURVIVAL
RAT-CATCHER
HOSTAGE

CHRIS RYAN

Mission: DESERT PURSUIT

05

03

02

01

00

ALPHA FORCE

RED FOX

ALPHA FORCE: DESERT PURSUIT
A RED FOX BOOK 0099 439263

First published in Great Britain by Red Fox,
an imprint of Random House Children's Books

This edition published 2004

Papers used by Random House Children's Books are natural, recyclable products made
from wood grown in sustainable forests. The manufacturing processes conform to the
environmental regulations of the country of origin.

Red Fox Books are published by Random House Children's Books,
61–63 Uxbridge Road, London W5 5SA,
a division of The Random House Group Ltd,
in Australia by Random House Australia (Pty) Ltd,
20 Alfred Street, Milsons Point, Sydney, NSW 2061, Australia,
in New Zealand by Random House New Zealand Ltd,
18 Poland Road, Glenfield, Auckland 10, New Zealand,
and in South Africa by Random House (Pty) Ltd,
Endulini, 5A Jubilee Road, Parktown 2193, South Africa

THE RANDOM HOUSE GROUP Limited Reg. No. 954009
www.kidsatrandomhouse.co.uk

A CIP catalogue record for this book is available from the British Library.

Set in 12/15 Palatino
Printed and bound in Great Britain by
Bookmarque Ltd, Croydon, Surrey

ALPHA FORCE

The field of operation...

SPAIN

MOROCCO TUNISIA

ISRAEL

WESTERN ALGERIA LIBYA

SAHARA EYGYPT

MAURITANIA MALI NIGER

One

The jerboa stopped in the sand-burrow entrance and peered out across the moonlit dune. It was summer in the Sahara Desert, when daytime temperatures above ground could reach a blistering fifty degrees Celsius, and the little rodent had slept away the hottest hours in the darkness of its burrow. Now, in the relative cool of the desert night, it was awake and hungry.

A beetle scuttled across the sand towards the burrow. The jerboa held still, waiting until the insect was within striking distance before springing forward with a powerful thrust of its long hind legs. It snatched up the beetle, bit off the snapping jaws and then settled back on its haunches to enjoy the meal. In common with most desert dwellers, the jerboa required very little water and the juicy innards of the beetle would provide all the fluid it needed.

Suddenly the jerboa stopped eating in mid-bite and sat upright, using its tufted tail for balance. It had heard something. Under its snout, the beetle's legs waved feebly, like a wind-blown moustache, but the jerboa remained frozen in place, listening intently. There were other things hunting in the dunes that night and survival meant staying alert. The sand began to vibrate as the sound grew louder, turning into a hum, then a high-pitched drone that seemed to come from everywhere at once.

The jerboa sprang for the safety of its burrow just as three quad bikes, each carrying two riders and pulling a small trailer, blasted over the crest of the dune. The combined engine noise briefly changed to a higher, whining note as the quads soared into the air, then gravity took over and the squat machines hit the downward slope with their heavily loaded trailers jouncing along behind them. The quads fish-tailed until the fat tyres got a grip, then they roared on down the dune slope in a shallow V formation, leaving three clouds of swirling sand in their wake. Alpha Force was in action.

They were travelling at night and off-road for a reason. Their mission was covert. They were in Western Sahara, a skinny little country wedged in next to Morocco on the Atlantic coast of north-western Africa. Western Sahara's recent history had been full of violence. Morocco had invaded, claiming that the country belonged to them, and the land had become a war zone as the people of Western Sahara, known as Sahawaris, fought a long, fierce guerrilla battle against the might of the Moroccan army. Now, many years after an uneasy ceasefire had been declared, some areas of Western Sahara were still dangerous. Morocco remained in control of the little country while, just over the border in Algeria, thousands of displaced Sahawaris lived in huge refugee camps.

Earlier that evening Alpha Force had slipped across the border from Algeria and now they were pushing further and further into territory that was patrolled by Moroccan troops. If they were discovered by the soldiers, their mission would be blown. To help them to remain invisible, the headlights of the three quad bikes were covered by infra-red filters. The drivers wore night-vision goggles and the lenses glowed like green insect eyes in the moonlight.

Paulo, the most experienced off-roader of them all, was in the lead. He had been riding quad bikes since he was eight years old. Back in Argentina, on his family cattle ranch, horses, 4x4s or quads were the only way to cross the huge expanses of rough ground in order to check on the stock. He had never driven in desert conditions before but he was learning fast and his face was set in a fierce grin as he reached the base of the dune and sent the quad bike leaping forward over the open ground ahead.

Alex was on Paulo's left flank. His shoulders were hunched and his thick, fair hair was dark with sweat as he struggled to match the speed of the lead quad. He had spent a few summers helping with the harvest on a farm near his home village in Northumberland, so he had some experience with tractors and quads, but he was nowhere near as expert as Paulo. They had been travelling for a good ten hours and his muscles were aching from the effort of keeping the quad on a steady course over the uneven ground, but the South American handled his machine with a casual ease, as though it were a part of him.

As he watched Paulo roar ahead, Alex clenched his jaw at the thought of coaxing even more speed out of his quad. Night-driving in the Sahara was tough on the nerves. The moonlight cast harsh, black shadows which played tricks with perspective. A shallow rut in the sand could look like a deep crevasse, but an axle-breaking trench might not show up until the last second. The night-vision goggles helped a lot, but Alex was still half-expecting to crash down into a hidden dry creek bed, known locally as a wadi, at any moment.

He sighed and took a firmer grip on the handlebars of

the quad, preparing to go for maximum speed. He knew Paulo was right to set such a demanding pace. There were only two hours left before dawn and Alpha Force had to reach their target zone before the sun was up. The sigh turned into a grunt as his passenger jabbed him sharply in the ribs.

'We're losing them, you idiot!' yelled Amber, her mouth five centimetres from his ear. 'C'mon! Put the pedal to the metal!'

Alex did the opposite. He slowed the quad to a stop, flipped up his night-vision goggles and turned to glare at Amber. His grey eyes were steely with annoyance but Amber did not flinch. She simply stared back, looking down her nose at him in her usual arrogant fashion as though he were an unsatisfactory chauffeur. Amber was in the habit of giving orders – and usually they were obeyed. She was a beautiful black American girl, the sole heir to a fortune which had come from a software empire worth billions of dollars. Her parents had died in a plane crash two years earlier and she now spent most of her days surrounded by people who were paid to look after her.

Alex was not one of those people. He and the rest of Alpha Force never allowed Amber to get away with rich-girl behaviour when she was with them.

'You think you can drive this thing faster than me?' asked Alex.

'Hell, yeah,' sniffed Amber.

'All right, then. You take over.'

Amber blinked in shock. She knew how to operate the quad, but she was uneasy around anything that had an engine. Yachts or horses were much more her style. 'I can't drive!' she spluttered. 'I – I mean, I'm the

4

navigator. I have to keep track of our route on the GPS system—'

'Then why don't you do that,' grated Alex, slamming the night-vision goggles back down over his eyes. 'And leave the driving to me?'

Amber looked solemnly into the round, green lenses of his goggles. 'OK, Kermit.'

Alex grinned despite himself, and Amber grinned back. Then the smile left her face as she glanced over Alex's shoulder. 'Quick!' she warned. 'They're changing direction!'

Alex turned to see the other two quads swinging right, towards a formation of dunes on the horizon. He realized that if he cut diagonally across the flat expanse of pebbly desert, he could gain some ground and catch up with them. Gritting his teeth, he opened up the throttle and the quad bike shot forward again.

It was Khalid who had told Paulo to turn east. Khalid was a twelve-year-old Sahawari boy from the refugee camp in Algeria, where they were based. He was acting as a guide for the mission and was riding behind Paulo on the lead quad. As soon as the dunes came into sight on the eastern horizon, he had tapped Paulo on the shoulder and indicated that they should head towards them. Paulo nodded to show that he understood and glanced over at the right-flanking quad to make sure Li had seen the signal too.

Li gave a thumbs-up sign, then peeled away in a turn so tight, it made her quad bike tip up on to the two right-side wheels. Smoothly, Li rose to her feet and leaned out to the left to provide counterbalance. Her long black hair feathered out behind her as she held the quad poised on two wheels, the trailer bouncing crazily along behind.

Hex, her passenger and the fifth member of Alpha Force, grabbed at the edges of his seat and hung on grimly.

'What the hell, Li!' he yelled.

'*Dios*,' muttered Paulo, watching Li's acrobatics with a mixture of worry and pride. He was more fond of the lively Anglo-Chinese girl than he cared to admit. This was her first time off-roading but she had taken to it like a natural. Years of training in martial arts and free climbing had given her a wiry strength, snake-fast reactions and a superb sense of balance, all of which came in very handy when driving a quad at full speed through the desert. On the down side, Li was also an adrenalin junkie, always looking for the next fix of excitement and with a bad habit of acting first and thinking later. If the quad bike tipped over, both she and Hex could be crushed under the heavy machine. Paulo turned his own quad and drew alongside her, shaking his head. Li grinned and deliberately kept her quad precariously balanced for a few more seconds before letting it settle back on to all four wheels.

As soon as the quad was stable again, Hex turned to make sure that a vital piece of equipment was still inside the trailer in its padded, hard-shelled case. He had wedged it in securely enough when they were loading up, but Li's extreme driving could dislodge an elephant. He spotted a corner of the polished steel container poking out under the covering tarpaulin and gave a relieved sigh. That piece of equipment was his responsibility and without it, the whole mission would fail.

Hex settled back into his seat and automatically checked the soft leather pouch that was strapped across his chest, inside his shirt. Tucked into the pouch was a hand-sized portable PC so technologically advanced it was not yet available on the open market. Hex grinned as he patted the leather pouch. Having a software billionaire as a friend did have some advantages. Hex was an expert hacker and code-breaker and the tiny PC was precious to him. After all, it contained most of his life. He lived in London, but the Net was his real home, and other hackers from the furthest corners of the world were closer to him than his own family.

As Hex felt the familiar shape of the palmtop under his hand, his fingers started jumping, tapping imaginary keys. When he was not on assignment with Alpha Force, Hex spent most of his spare time on the Net and now he was suffering withdrawal symptoms. His green eyes narrowed into disgusted slits as he scanned the Saharan landscape. Other people saw a stark beauty in the desert but Hex saw only millions of grains of sand, any one of which might work its gritty way into his state-of-the-art palmtop and cripple the delicate electronics. Hex was no couch potato – his body was firm and muscled as a result of regular trips to the gym – but he had never understood why some people loved the great outdoors.

'I hate it,' he said, without realizing he had spoken aloud.

'What?' called Li over her shoulder.

'Outside,' shouted Hex, putting a protective hand over his palmtop as Alex and Amber caught up and cut across their path, sending a stinging spray of pebbly grit into the air. 'I hate it!'

Alex took up his original position on Paulo's left flank and Alpha Force continued on their way, speeding through the night, racing to beat the sun. Ahead of them loomed the black silhouettes of the dunes, their mission destination.

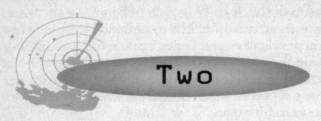

TWO

The dune towered above Alpha Force as they stood in a tired huddle, stretching their aching muscles. They had reached the target zone. It had been a hard journey and they were glad to be off the quads at last. The machines and their trailers were parked neatly in a row at the base of the dune and the ticking of their cooling engines was loud in the silence of the desert.

Alex moved around the group, pouring water from the jerry can he had unloaded from one of the trailers. For a moment no-one spoke as they all drank thirstily and then held out their beakers for refills. Travelling at night meant that they had not been faced with the roasting desert sun, or the drying wind that always started up at sunrise. In fact, the night-time temperature had been a reasonable thirty degrees Celsius, but still they were all feeling dehydrated. They were dressed properly for the desert in gandourah and sirwal, and the flowing shirts and baggy trousers gave some protection against water loss through evaporation, but their bodies were still adapting to the arid conditions and at the end of the journey only Khalid had seemed unaffected by thirst. Alex shook his head in admiration as he remembered how the Sahawari boy had casually turned down the offered water before loping off into the darkness to scout the area.

'We made it,' sighed Paulo, once he had drained his second cup of water.

'Only just,' said Li, nodding at the sky. Behind the top of the dune, the first streaks of crimson were beginning to show in the east.

'Hex, how much light are you going to need for the next phase of the mission?' asked Alex.

'It has to be full daylight for the best results,' said Hex.

'That's still a few hours away,' judged Li.

'Until then, we shall be well hidden here, yes?' asked Paulo.

Amber nodded. 'Khalid told me the army patrols keep to the road unless they see anything suspicious. As long as we stay on the western side of the dune, we're out of sight of the road.'

'We should still pitch the camouflage awnings,' said Alex. 'Just in case they have helicopters or something. The awnings'll give us shade, too. This hollow is going to turn into an oven once the sun climbs above the dune.'

He glanced around at the others, waiting for their agreement. In the red light of dawn, they looked as tired as he felt and he knew they must be tempted to simply curl up in the warm sand and go to sleep. He certainly was. His muscles felt as though they had been put through a shredding machine and his head was still full of the whining drone of quad engines.

'You survival experts. *So* boring,' sighed Li, sending Alex a mischievous sideways glance from her uptilted eyes. 'Do this. Do that. Always planning ahead. Can't you, just for once, live in the moment?'

'If you want to survive—' began Alex.

'—you have to be prepared,' finished Li, crossing her eyes comically.

Paulo laughed at Li, then raked his dark curls back from his forehead and assumed a serious expression. 'The four elements of survival are—'

'—shelter, water, food, fire,' recited Amber, Li, Paulo and Hex in perfect unison.

'Well, they are!' said Alex, trying to look offended. 'But not necessarily in that order. The thing is,' he continued, in a deadpan, lecturing tone, 'you have to take account of your environment—'

He broke off as the others scattered, heading for the trailers and leaving him standing on his own.

'No, listen,' he continued as he followed them. 'This is really interesting . . .'

Four plastic beakers flew through the air, aimed directly at his head. Alex dodged them easily, then began helping to unload the trailers with a broad grin on his face. He had hardly seen the others since Christmas, when they had spent a couple of weeks on Paulo's ranch after completing a successful mission in Ecuador, and it felt good to be part of a team again.

They worked well together, moving quietly and efficiently to erect the awnings over the quads and trailers. The desert camouflage colours would hide the machines from all but the closest inspection. The awnings had a skeleton of fibreglass poles which, once assembled, kept them rigid and anchored. Within fifteen minutes the quads and trailers were hidden under the awnings and there was enough space around the machines for six people to stretch out in the shade.

Once the trailers were unloaded and the awnings in place, the team split up. Paulo overhauled the quads, checking oil and water and topping up the fuel. The

10

machines had to be primed and ready in case a quick escape was needed.

Alex and Li set up the stove and started preparing a meal. It was against all Alex's instincts to use the stove. He would much prefer to light a fire. He had his survival tin in his belt pouch, with his knife in a sheath beside it. Normally, that was all he ever needed, but fuel was scarce in the desert and, at least with the stove, there would be no tell-tale smoke to give away their position.

Hex sat down with his palmtop. His task was to send a progress report back to their base in Algeria. The flat aerial in the lid of the palmtop meant that he could connect with the nearest communications satellite and then surf the Net from anywhere in the world.

Amber unclipped the three GPS units from the handle-bars of the quads and sat down cross-legged on the sand with the small black boxes laid out in front of her. They looked a bit like calculators with oversized display panels, but they were a lot more sophisticated than that. The initials GPS stood for global positioning systems, which meant that the units used satellite technology to navigate with pinpoint accuracy anywhere in the world.

There had been very few landmarks along the route they had taken that night, but every time Amber had spotted one she had carefully stored it as a waypoint in the memory of her quad's GPS unit. Now she needed to key the same information into the other two GPS units. That way, if the quads became separated for any reason, the drivers would each be able to find their way back over the border into Algeria by using the GPS back-tracking facility.

Amber switched on all three GPS units, then sat back to wait while they locked on to the NAVSTAR system, a network of twenty-four satellites owned and operated by the US military. Once the units were receiving signals from three or four of the satellites, then they would be ready to give an accurate position, but it usually took a couple of minutes to get a fix. While she waited, Amber looked across at Hex. He was hunched over his palmtop and his fingers were flying across the keys at such a speed, they were only a blur. Her face creased into an affectionate smile. As a rule, she would rather die than let Hex see her looking at him with anything but disdain, but once he was on the Net he was lost to the world. A herd of stampeding camels could race through the camp and he would not even glance up from the screen.

'You like him?' said a soft voice behind her.

Amber jumped and twisted round in the sand, her eyes wide with shock. She was holding one of the GPS units in her hand and, in the green light thrown out from the little screen, a face from a horror movie loomed into view. The lips were pulled back in a lopsided grimace and the whole of one side of the face, from chin to brow, was a mass of shiny, puckered scar tissue. The ear was a shrivelled stump and the scalp surrounding it was hairless and pulled tight against the skull.

Amber gave a low, frightened scream and dropped the GPS unit. As soon as the green light from the screen was gone, the horror mask rearranged itself into the familiar, scarred features of Khalid, their young guide. He had made his way back into the camp so silently, no-one had heard him arrive. Instantly, Amber regretted her scream, but Khalid's lopsided grin remained in place. He was not at all self-conscious about his mangled face. It had been with him since he was a baby, strapped to his mother's back as she and his father cleared the ground around their date palms. They had returned to their home in Western Sahara after the ceasefire had been declared and had begun to reclaim the overgrown oasis, but they had disturbed a buried landmine. Khalid's father and mother had both been killed. He had been protected from the blast by his mother's body, except for the left half of his face, which had been peeping over her shoulder as she bent to her work. This was partly why thousands of Sahawari refugees remained in the camps in Algeria, despite the ceasefire. Their homeland was sown with thousands upon thousands of landmines.

It was also the reason why Alpha Force was in Western Sahara that night.

'Khalid! Don't creep up on me like that!' hissed Amber, putting her hand to her heart. 'You scared me.'

'You like him?' repeated Khalid teasingly, in the broken English he had picked up from the foreign aid workers in the refugee camp. Like most Arabs living in Algeria, French was his second language, but he preferred to practise his English when he had the chance.

'Hex? Are you kidding? Perlease . . .'

'I think answer is yes,' grinned Khalid.

Amber could feel a blush spreading across her face and frantically searched around for something to say. Alex, Paulo and Li were already listening with amused interest. She had to change the subject before Hex tuned into the conversation.

'So, is it all quiet out there?' she asked, busying herself with the GPS units.

'All is quiet,' said Khalid.

'In that case,' said Alex, casually getting to his feet, 'I'm just going to have a quick look up top.'

'Not further than top,' warned Khalid. 'Is danger further.'

'Not further,' promised Alex. He looked over at Hex, but Hex was still lost on the Net. He shrugged and looked over at Paulo. 'Coming?'

Paulo nodded and grabbed two sets of night-vision goggles from the quads. He handed one pair to Alex and they made their way over to the base of the dune.

'Ready?' asked Paulo.

Alex nodded. 'Let's get it over with.'

Three

Hex hardly glanced up from his palmtop as they started to climb, but Li, Amber and Khalid all stopped what they were doing to watch. Their faces were serious as they followed Alex and Paulo's slow progress up the steep slope. They all knew what was waiting on the other side of the dune.

When Alex and Paulo reached the top, they went down on to their bellies and crawled the last couple of metres. Khalid had said it was all quiet, but that was no reason to carelessly skyline themselves. Once they were in position, they both lowered the night-vision goggles over their eyes. They lay there in silence for a few minutes, taking in the scene below, then Alex tapped Paulo on the shoulder and they wriggled down the slope until it was safe to stand again. Their faces were grim as they flipped up the goggles and shared a look before turning to begin the trek back down.

'Still there?' asked Li, when Alex and Paulo arrived back at the base of the dune.

'Still there,' said Alex briefly, heading for the stove to check on the progress of the boil-in-the bag meals he and Li were preparing. Paulo took the night-vision goggles back to the quads and began stowing away the jerry cans of fuel, oil and water he had been using. Amber watched them both for a moment, but neither of them said any more. She looked at their grim faces and bit back the questions she wanted to ask. They would talk when they were ready.

She returned to her work on the GPS units and Khalid settled down to watch her. He was fascinated with them, but Amber was more impressed with Khalid's navigational skills. She considered herself to be a pretty expert navigator, but Khalid's ability to find his way through almost featureless desert without a map or compass was way beyond her capabilities.

'Tell me how you found your way here tonight, Khalid,' she said.

'The stars,' said Khalid.

'Yeah, yeah, that's fine as a basic direction finder, but how do you find your way right to this particular dune? They all look the same to me.'

'We leave, how you say, signs?'

'Markers?'

Khalid nodded. 'We put stones.'

'In piles? Cairns?'

Khalid nodded again.

'A bit like this,' said Amber, holding out one of the GPS units so that Khalid could watch what she was doing. 'I've put electronic markers on to this, see? That one there, that's the location for the ruined fort we passed. And that's the position of the big oasis we could see on the horizon. Do you know the one I mean?'

Khalid's lopsided smile disappeared. He nodded and looked away.

'What?' asked Amber. 'What is it?'

'My family.'

'That was the oasis where they died? I'm sorry, Khalid. My parents are dead too, you know. They were killed in a plane crash. I should have been on the plane with them, but I changed my mind at the last minute. It was sabotage. Do you know what that means?'

Khalid nodded. 'Why?'

'They were secretly involved in some very dangerous stuff,' said Amber. 'They wanted to help people, you see. People too poor or trapped to help themselves. They wanted to make a difference – something more than just giving money away. They worked undercover all over the world. They put themselves in danger and made some very nasty enemies and then—' Amber shrugged and gave Khalid a wobbly smile – 'and then, one of their enemies decided to stop them.'

'And now, you do same as parents?' asked Khalid.

'We all do,' said Li, sitting down beside Amber.

'That's why Philippe called us in,' said Hex, closing the lid of his palmtop and coming to join them.

'Ah! Dr Philippe!' smiled Khalid, his eyes shining. Philippe Larousse was his hero. He was a French plastic surgeon who came to Khalid's refugee camp every year to work with landmine victims. He had been at the camp eleven years earlier, when the baby Khalid had been brought in after the explosion. Philippe had saved both his life and the sight in his left eye. He looked around the group, eager for any details about his hero. 'How you meet Dr Philippe?'

'You could say Philippe was there at the start of Alpha Force,' said Alex, bringing over the hot food.

Paulo followed after him, hungrily sniffing the air. 'We were all stranded on an Indonesian island and, well—'

'—we saved his life,' finished Amber proudly.

'You save Dr Philippe? Then my life is yours,' vowed Khalid, looking at Alpha Force with a new respect.

17

Nobody quite knew what to say to that. Paulo looked at the young boy's serious face and rubbed his nose in embarrassment. 'Let us eat,' he said, taking one of the mess cans of food.

'Don't ask me what it is,' warned Alex, handing out the other mess cans. 'It's brown and it's hot. That's about all I can tell you.'

By the time they had all finished eating, the sky was growing lighter by the second. It was time to retreat under the shade of the awnings and try to snatch some sleep. But first they needed to talk about the next phase of the mission. Hex unloaded the polished steel case from the quad trailer and carried it over to the circle, where everyone was looking expectantly at Alex and Paulo. The two boys glanced at one another and Paulo nodded. Alex took a deep breath and started to describe what he and Paulo had seen on the other side of the dune.

'OK. It's exactly as Khalid described. There's a defensive berm running east to west.'

'What is berm?' said Khalid, looking puzzled.

'That's military-speak for a wall,' explained Li, giving Alex a withering look. 'He does that a lot. His dad's in the SAS, you see, and it rubs off on him.'

'Sorry,' said Alex. 'Wall. There's a massive, defensive earth wall, built by the Moroccans during the war. It's fortified with razor wire and mines. The ground between the wall and this dune is also, as we know, sown with mines. It's flat, stony ground. About halfway across is where . . .' Alex hesitated and glanced at Khalid.

'Where my friends are?' asked Khalid.

'Yes. Your friends. They're about halfway across. Two of them. Two bodies.'

Two bodies. There was a silence as the reality of their mission in Western Sahara hit home. It had all started a few weeks earlier, when the Sahawari refugees in Algeria had heard that the Moroccans were inviting a multinational oil company into Western Sahara to look for oil. The news had been too much for one group of older Sahawari boys, who were already feeling rebellious and unhappy with their life in the camps. The boys had cooked up a plan to draw attention to the situation, which involved going into Western Sahara, defusing landmines and then bringing them back across the border. The boys had planned on using the explosive charges from the mines to blow a hole in the supply pipe from one of the oil company's installations in Algeria, but the plan had gone horribly wrong. Two of the boys had been killed outright in the Western Saharan minefield and the other three had staggered back into the refugee camp two days later, suffering from shock and dehydration.

Philippe Larousse had called in Alpha Force because he suspected that the remaining three boys were planning to try again. Once Alpha Force had arrived in the camp and seen the boys' secretive, sullen faces, they had been forced to agree with Philippe's assessment.

'And this will stop them?' asked Khalid, gazing at the metal case Hex was cradling.

'Should do,' said Hex, flipping open the case. 'Your friends want to blow up the pipeline to get publicity for the Sahawari refugees. But if we get their publicity for them, then they won't need to risk their lives playing with landmines.' Hex eased a digital camcorder from the case and began to check it over. 'We'll film what happened here and get it out to every news station we can think of. That should keep your friends happy.'

'Why are the bodies still there?' demanded Amber. 'Why haven't the soldiers removed them?'

'Well, for one thing, they may not have been noticed,' said Alex. 'There are other craters, other bodies out there. Animals that wandered on to the minefield.'

'But surely they can tell the difference between people and animals?' asked Li.

Alex and Paulo shared a look but said nothing.

'That bad?' asked Hex softly.

Li crossed her arms and stared at Alex. 'We should do it.'

'Retrieve the bodies?' Alex shook his head. 'Sorry, Li. If they'd been at the edge of the minefield, maybe. But they're too far in.'

'We should've brought a metal detector,' said Amber.

'Wouldn't work,' said Hex. 'Mines are made out of plastic these days. Harder to detect.'

'But we can't just leave the bodies there to rot,' pleaded Li. 'Isn't there some way we can reach them?'

'Li,' sighed Hex. 'When I was on the Net earlier, I found out more than I ever wanted to know about landmines. You'd be less keen to go out there if you knew what these things can do to a person—'

'Go on, then,' said Li defiantly. 'Tell me.'

Hex gave her a level stare, then began quoting word for word from the last website he had visited. '"A mine contains extremely explosive material that creates a wall of air and debris that expands outward at almost seven thousand metres per second. Some mines have metal projectiles inside, such as ball-bearings or nails, that puncture soft flesh and shred bones into a fine spray. The shock waves are so strong that many victims find their feet still in their boots, while splinters of their shin bones are blasted deep into the flesh of other victims. If you don't die of blast injuries, blood loss or shock, then massive infection will result from all the dirt that the explosion has blasted into you and-"'

'That is enough, I think,' said Paulo quietly. He put his arm around Li's shoulders and she hid her face against his chest.

Hex shrugged and sat back. He had made his point.

Alex got to his feet. 'We're all tired. We need sleep. In a few hours' time we'll do what we have to do and get out of here before the first patrol shows up. Job done. Simple.'

The rest of Alpha Force nodded agreement. Get the job done and get out. Simple. What could possibly go wrong?

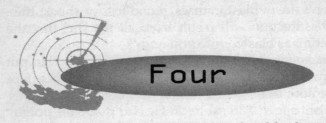

Four

Hex slung the camcorder over his shoulder by its strap and squinted up at the top of the dune, shading his eyes against the glare. Alpha Force had delayed climbing the dune for as long as they dared, to get the best light for filming, but it was after nine o'clock now and the sun was high in the sky. Khalid was already in look-out position, lying on his belly at the highest point of the dune and watching the road beyond the berm. Hex waited until Khalid turned and gave him a thumbs-up signal, which meant there were no patrols in sight.

'Ready?' said Hex, looking enquiringly at the others.

'Let's do it,' said Li.

The smell hit them when they were nearly at the top of the slope. It came from the other side of the dune, carried on the hot, desert wind that had started with the sunrise. One by one they came to a halt, digging the toes of their boots into the steep slope to make footholds in the sand. Their faces were grim as they looked at one another. They knew what the sweet, meaty smell was. It was the odour of rotting flesh.

'That is so gross,' said Amber faintly, turning her back to the wind.

As protection against the sun, they were all wearing layered headcloths, wrapped around their heads and faces in the desert way. Amber pulled her headcloth more tightly across her face so that only her big, dark eyes were showing. It made no difference and she retched as the thick smell coated the back of her throat.

'You don't have to go any further,' said Hex, pulling his own cloth across his nose.

'Or you, Li,' said Paulo.

The colour had left Li's high cheekbones, but her eyes above the headcloth were determined. 'Hey! We're all in this together,' she protested, turning back to the climb.

They went down on their bellies and commando-crawled the last couple of metres to the top. One by one they propped themselves up on their elbows and silently looked down on the dreadful scene below. Hex lifted the camcorder, adjusted the focus and began to film the bodies in close-up.

The first boy lay on his back where the blast had thrown him. He was staring sightlessly into the burning desert sun and his open mouth was full of sand. His legs ended at the knees in tatters of ragged flesh, but that was not what had killed him. A splinter of metal had pierced his eye, driving deep into his brain. There was no blood. The sand had soaked most of it up and the sun had dried the rest. Hex kept the camera on the body for as long as he could, turning away only when a centipede slithered from the boy's ear.

The second boy was a few metres away, face down. He had fallen on top of another mine and the explosion had blasted him apart. There was not much left to show that the scattered remains had once been a person. Hex swallowed hard and held the camcorder steady while he silently counted to ten, then he pulled back for a wide shot of the desolation of razor wire and churned-up earth. All the while, the others lay alongside him, silent witnesses to the pointless deaths of two young boys.

Hex stopped filming and played back the footage to make sure it was good. The camcorder had caught every detail. He slipped the tiny DV tape cassette out of the camcorder, stowed it in a protective wallet and stashed it safely in the leather pouch that held his palmtop.

'That's it,' he said finally. 'We're done—'

At that instant, Li jumped to her feet with a wordless cry, pointing at the sky. They all followed her shaking finger and saw three dark shapes circling above the minefield, their broad, ragged wings spread wide to catch the thermals that came with the heat of the day. Vultures. The three huge birds began to spiral lazily downwards as the rest of Alpha Force scrambled to their feet and looked on in horror.

The vultures landed on the bodies, holding their wings aloft to protect their share and hissing evilly at one another. Paulo groaned and turned away as one bird thrust its naked head and neck deep into the chest cavity of one of the boys and tore away a chunk of flesh with its heavy, sharply hooked beak. The boy twitched and his arms flopped as though he were trying to get up.

'I can't watch any more,' said Amber. 'Can we go now?'

Sickened, they turned away, ready to head back down the slope, but Li suddenly launched herself out onto the minefield side of the dune and ran with floundering strides down the steep slope. As she ran, she waved her arms above her head and yelled at the top of her voice, trying to scare the birds off. The vultures barely moved. Li was too far away from them to pose a threat.

Khalid shouted a warning, his voice high with panic, but Li ignored him.

'*Dios*,' breathed Paulo. He turned, ready to launch himself after Li, but Alex grabbed him round the legs and brought him down in a rugby-style tackle.

'Li!' shrieked Amber. 'Stop! You have to stop! The mines!'

Li seemed to come to her senses. She leaned back and dug in her heels, trying to slow her descent, but she was going too fast. She careered down to the bottom of the dune slope, coming to a stop only as the ground levelled out. There, she stared at the birds for a few more seconds while the others held their breath, then her shoulders slumped in defeat. She turned and began trudging back up the slope towards them.

Alex gave a relieved sigh and let go of Paulo.

Paulo scrambled to his feet, shaking his head. Under his tan, the blood had drained away from his face so completely, he looked almost green. 'That girl,' he said. 'She is mad. Does she stop to think? No! She just—'

'—jumps in,' finished Amber, nodding in heartfelt agreement. 'Yeah, well, I'm gonna give her something to think about when she gets back up here—'

'She's stopped,' said Hex.

They all turned to look at Li. She had come to a sudden halt a third of the way up the slope and was standing, head down and motionless, with her left foot suspended centimetres above the sand.

'What is she doing now?' demanded Amber. 'Honestly, I . . .'

Her words faded away as Li slowly, carefully, raised her head and looked up at them. There was no mistaking the expression on her face. It was sheer terror.

Hex lifted the camcorder to his eye and zoomed in on Li's foot. 'Oh, no,' he breathed, as he saw the taut length of shimmering, silver wire that she had hooked out of the sand with the toe of her boot. It was caught under one of the little metal tabs that held her bootlaces in place.

'What is it?' asked Paulo.

'Tripwire,' said Hex briefly.

'*Dios*,' breathed Paulo. Of all of them, he was closest to Li and his hands clenched into fists at the thought of her ending up like the two boys in the minefield.

'What do we do?' whispered Amber. 'What can we do?'

Paulo looked down the slope, directly into Li's terrified eyes, and he forced himself to smile reassuringly. 'Good girl, Li. You are doing exactly the right thing. Stay as still as you can. We will get you out of there.'

'She can't stay motionless for long!' hissed Amber. 'Not on a forty-five-degree slope! What do we do?'

'Hex?' said Alex. 'Can you help?'

Hex waved away the question. He was already deep in thought, going through all the landmine information he had picked up on the Net a few hours earlier. Hex had a photographic memory, so if he had read anything about tripwire mines, he would be able to retrieve it. All he had to do was find the right file.

'Got it!' he said, lifting his head. 'It's probably one of the M2 series. They're nasty. A type of bounding, fragmentation mine.'

'What does that mean?' asked Paulo with an anguished glance down the slope to Li.

'When the tripwire is triggered, the mine fires a sort of grenade two metres into the air. The grenade explodes, blasting shrapnel at everything around it.'

'Do you know how to defuse it?' asked Alex.

Hex brought the relevant page up on the screen inside his head. He scanned the information there, then nodded. 'In theory,' he said. 'We're going to need some pliers.'

Paulo patted the tool-pouch at his belt. 'I have them. Let us go.'

'Wait,' said Hex. 'Before anyone goes down there, I want to make sure we're all clear about this. The mine on the end of that tripwire jumps into the air before it explodes. So, if things turn bad, Li won't be the only one to die. Understand?'

'I understand,' said Paulo. 'Now, can we go?'

Hex and Paulo set off down the slope, treading slowly and carefully in Li's footprints. They were the logical choices – Hex had the knowledge and Paulo had the tools and the skill to use them – but still, Alex and Amber found it hard to stay back and watch. Khalid joined them at the top of the dune and the three of them lay belly down on the western slope, peering over the crest of the dune, willing the rescue to go well.

As Paulo got closer to Li, he could see the strain on her face as she struggled to stay balanced on the steep slope. Her muscles were extremely strong from years of free climbing, but already there was a slight tremor in the leg that was holding all her weight.

'Don't touch me,' she begged, in a high-pitched, panicky voice. 'And don't make the sand move.'

'Not going to,' said Hex calmly as he stepped over to the left in front of Li. He placed his feet with great care, making sure the sand was not going to shift before he put his full weight on the slope. Once he was sure the sand was stable, he eased down into a kneeling position.

Paulo slowly moved into place on his right, hunkering down on his haunches so that Li's foot, and the tripwire, were directly in front of him. His heart sank when he saw how firmly the wire was caught in the metal laces tab. There was no way they could release it without tripping the detonator.

'OK, Li,' said Hex. 'I'm not going to touch you, but if you want, you can use my shoulder to lean on.'

'You won't move?' quavered Li.

'Me? Steady as a rock.'

Li lifted her hand, hesitated, then reached out and gripped Hex's shoulder, digging her fingers in hard enough to make him wince.

'Do not worry, Li,' said Paulo. 'Hex knows how to make this mine safe. Right, Hex?'

'Right. First, we need to make sure it's the type I think it is. Paulo, I want you to dig down into the sand about ten centimetres to the right. We're looking for a black tube, the size and shape of a large torch, with a separate, smaller pipe sticking up alongside it, attached at the base. If you uncover any part of the tripwire, you have to stop immediately – and I mean immediately. The tripwire must not move. Cover it up again and start digging a bit further over.'

Paulo worked in silence, painstakingly moving the sand a handful at a time. Hex kneeled, staying as still as he could to support Li. The sun burned down on their backs and the sweat poured out of them, evaporating instantly where their skin was exposed and leaving behind a fine, white residue of salt.

Finally, Paulo sat back on his haunches. 'Hex,' he said, his voice tight with tension. 'I have found something.'

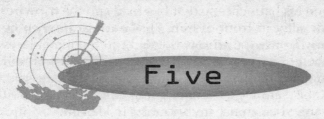

Five

Paulo leaned back to let Hex see the top of a black tube, with a smaller pipe periscoping out of the sand beside it.

'Good,' said Hex, injecting as much confidence into his voice as he could. 'Just as I thought. Don't touch anything yet, Paulo. Li, when you're ready, I want you to let go of my shoulder and lean on Paulo instead. I need to dig this side now.'

'But, I have found the mine, yes?' said Paulo.

'Yeah, but sometimes these tripwires have two nasty surprises – one on each end.'

Hex waited patiently until Li felt confident enough to switch shoulders, then he started digging.

'Paulo,' whispered Li, 'I – I don't know how much longer I can hold still.'

Paulo looked up at her. Two tears were trickling down her cheeks and her head was beginning to tremble on her neck.

'You will be fine,' he said, looking her in the eye.

'Yes, I'll be fine,' whispered Li. 'But . . . just in case, if I tell you both to get out of here, you have to go. Promise me you'll go.'

'Stop being so noble,' said Paulo with a grin.

'Got it,' said Hex, as his fingers came up against a hard, rough surface. Gently, he brushed the sand away, then sat back on his heels with a relieved sigh. His end of the tripwire was wrapped around nothing more than a large rock.

'Now, all we have to do is make the mine safe without tripping the wire,' said Hex lightly.

Paulo grinned at him and took out the customized tool-kit he carried in his belt pouch. 'Let us start,' he said.

At the top of the dune, Amber nudged Alex impatiently. 'Why have they stopped digging?' she demanded.

Alex frowned into the camcorder, adjusting the focus slightly. 'Looks like they've uncovered the mine.'

'Let me see!' Amber snatched the camcorder away from Alex. He sighed and lifted his head to ease the tension in his neck. Since Hex and Paulo had started digging, every second had seemed to last a minute. As he stretched his neck, a bright flash from the road on the other side of the berm caught his eye. Alex looked across, then snatched the camcorder back, ignoring Amber's protests. He focused on the road and what he saw there made his heart sink. The bright flash he had seen was the sun bouncing off the windscreen of an approaching vehicle. A jeep. A military jeep.

'What is it?' asked Amber.

'Army patrol,' said Alex. 'And they're heading this way.'

'See those three prongs sticking out of the top of the smaller pipe?' asked Hex.

Paulo nodded.

'The pipe is called a flash tube. The three prongs are the top part of the fuse,' said Hex. 'If I'm right, there's a hole through the flash tube just under the sand there. The tripwire is attached to a release pin which fits into

30

that hole. When the wire is tripped, it yanks the pin out of the hole. That releases a spring-loaded striker—'

'—which sets off the mine,' finished Paulo.

'Yeah. Now, when Li tripped the wire, she must only have pulled the pin part of the way out. What you have to do is clear the sand away and push the release pin all the way back into the hole. When you're sure it's secure, then you can cut the wire with the pliers.'

'That is it? But it is so simple,' said Paulo, smiling up at Li.

'In theory, yes,' said Hex reluctantly. 'But what we don't know is how much of the pin is still left in the hole. It could be hanging by a thread. Even the slightest disturbance could—'

'Hex!' called Alex softly from the top of the dune. 'Patrol on the way. ETA three to four minutes.'

Li gave a strangled sob and the foot that had snagged the wire wobbled dangerously.

'Be still!' snapped Paulo. 'Forget the soldiers. We are doing this. Only this.'

Li gulped and nodded, holding her leg as still as she could and trying to ignore the excruciating cramps that were twisting through her thigh muscles. Paulo leaned forward and began to move the sand from around the flash tube. His big hands worked with delicacy and confidence and soon he could see the gleam of the wire through the sand. He stopped, leaned forward and gently blew the last of the sand away. As he did so, the sound of a jeep engine carried on the wind. The patrol was nearly upon them.

Up on the top of the dune, Alex, Amber and Khalid ducked low as the jeep came into view on the road.

31

'Khalid, run. Hide!' ordered Amber.

Khalid shook his head.

'You must get out of here!' insisted Amber. 'If the troops find us five, it's no big deal. We're just a bunch of stupid tourist kids who lost our way. But if they catch you, you'll end up in prison!'

'I stay,' said Khalid. 'I am guide. Only I know safe way back.'

'I have the GPS, remember?'

'Do this GPS show hiding mines?'

Amber glared at Khalid. He stared back calmly, his dark eyes stubborn and determined in his ruin of a face, and all the while the noise of the jeep engine grew louder.

'I can see the pin,' said Paulo.

'Can you get hold of it?' asked Hex.

Paulo reached forward to grasp the pin, then hesitated, frightened of knocking it from the hole. His hand hovered uncertainly and Li's foot twitched again as a particularly bad cramp bit into her leg. The wire jumped, yanking the pin and Paulo lunged. He nipped the pin between his thumb and forefinger just before the last few millimetres slid from the hole.

For one second, two, he was frozen in place, waiting for the explosion. When nothing happened, he slowly slid the pin back through the hole in the flash tube. Once it was in, he picked up the pliers and clipped the wire.

Li collapsed to her knees and covered her face with her hands.

'Let's go!' yelled Paulo.

'Come on,' said Hex, putting an arm around Li's shaking shoulders and dragging her to her feet. 'No time for that. We have to get out of here.'

Hex half-dragged Li up the slope as the jeep came to a stop on the other side of the berm. They were still in full view and in another few seconds the soldiers would be out of the jeep and climbing the metal steps to the observation platform that was built into the berm.

Amber, Alex and Khalid were already running down the other side of the dune, heading for the quads. Hex and Li reached the top and plunged after them without looking back. Paulo watched them go, making sure Li was out of harm's way before he looked down once more at the little pin he was still holding in place with his finger. He had known straight away that the pin was unstable. The mine was tilted to one side and, without the sand packed around it, the pin was likely to slip out as soon as he let go of it.

Paulo heard the sound of booted feet clanging on metal and then men's voices talking and laughing. The soldiers were climbing the steps to the observation platform and he was still in full view on the dune slope. Quickly, Paulo scooped a wall of sand around the pin and patted it into place, but the fine, dry grains of sand had nothing to hold them together and the wall started to crumble away almost immediately. Paulo groaned, then let go of the pin. Without stopping to see what happened he surged to his feet and powered up the slope. He was still a metre away from the dune crest when he heard a sharp, metallic click.

The pin had fallen out, releasing the striker mechanism.

With a yell, Paulo launched himself over the crest of the dune as a fist of air hit him in the back. A split second later, the noise of the explosion blasted his eardrums and a geyser of sand erupted, rising high above the top of the dune. Then he was rolling down the far slope of the dune, falling out of control, head over heels.

The soldiers had just reached the observation platform when the mine exploded. They ducked instinctively. One flung himself down on to the platform, then climbed to his feet again a couple of seconds later, grinning shamefacedly. They looked for the cause of the explosion and spotted the three vultures, climbing into the sky in a panic of flapping wings. Satisfied, the soldiers turned away and headed back to the shelter of their jeep, hooking their cigarettes from their shirt pockets as they went. This was a routine patrol in a quiet area and they did not intend to stand out in the desert sun for long. None of them had spotted the bodies of the two boys lying out on the minefield, half-hidden by razor wire and churned-up earth.

Paulo staggered to his feet at the bottom of the western slope as sand and small stones rained down all around him. His ears were ringing painfully but, to his surprise, he seemed to be all in one piece. Dizzily, he looked over at the quads. The others were mounted and ready to go. They were waving him on and their mouths were moving as they yelled encouragement, but he could not hear a thing. Paulo headed for the nearest quad at a stumbling run and climbed on behind Hex.

'Let's get out of here!' called Alex.

The three quads blasted out from under the camouflage awnings and headed off at high speed with their trailers bouncing crazily. Three minutes later they rounded the shoulder of another dune and disappeared from sight, leaving nothing but a trail of settling dust behind them.

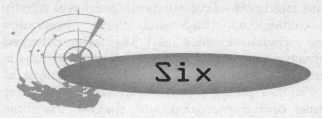

Six

In the early dawn light the huge, dusty refugee camp sprawled in the middle of a plain of dark, featureless sand. The only splash of colour came from the black, white, green and red flags that fluttered from the tent masts, and the only sound was the snap of canvas in the fierce, gusting wind. Alpha Force grinned at one another as they headed across the plain towards the camp. It might look bleak but it was a welcome sight. The previous day, once they were sure they had not been followed by the Moroccan soldiers, they had waited for the cool of the night before travelling back to the camp. Now they were tired and hungry and looking forward to a wash and a change of clothes.

As they reached the outskirts of the camp, the packed-earth roads between the tents and mud-brick huts were empty, but the whine of their quad engines brought heads popping from doorways and children tumbling out into the dust. Soon their arrival had turned into a noisy procession and they had to slow the quads to a careful crawl to avoid squashing small children under their wheels.

Khalid climbed down from the back of Alex's quad and walked along, waving and smiling like a returning hero. The camp was divided into six villages, or darias, and this was his home daria. He was well known and loved here, and nobody noticed his scarred face. The sad fact was that Khalid was not unusual. There were plenty of other Sahawaris with landmine injuries. The smaller children especially loved Khalid. They were clustered around him now, hanging from his arms and clinging to his gandourah. Khalid bore it all with a broad grin on his face.

Minutes later, they arrived in the main square at the centre of the daria. In the middle was the all-important water cistern, which supplied the whole daria; around the edge a row of low, mud-brick buildings housed a primary school, a crèche, a dispensary and a hospital. As Alpha Force turned off their engines and climbed tiredly from the quads, the hospital doors flew open and Philippe Larousse hurried out, closely followed by a tall black man in western clothes who was checking them over for injuries before he was even out of the doorway. This was John Middleton, Amber's uncle, who acted as a financier, organizer and anchor man for Alpha Force, as he had done for Amber's parents before they were killed.

'Hi,' said Amber, smiling at his anxious face. 'Don't worry, Uncle. We're all back in one piece.'

'No problems, then?' asked Jack Middleton, looking from Amber to Paulo, who was standing next to her.

'What?' shouted Paulo.

'I said, did you have any problems?'

'What?' shouted Paulo again.

'Is he OK?' asked John Middleton, giving Amber a questioning look.

'Wha-?' Paulo's third shout ended abruptly in a grunt as Amber dug her elbow into his ribs.

'Sand in his ears, probably,' Amber lied. She knew

that Paulo was still suffering from the after-effects of the landmine explosion, but she had no intention of telling her uncle about that particular incident. When they had all first come up with the idea of forming Alpha Force, John Middleton had been very reluctant to agree to it and she did not want to give him any reason to change his mind.

Just then a tall, imposing Sahawari woman walked into the square. Her brightly coloured malaafa robe covered most of her head and body, but her dark eyes, her straight back, even the way she moved, were all full of a quiet authority. She was the head of the daria and everyone, even the chattering toddlers, grew silent as she approached. Beside her walked the parents of the two dead Sahawari boys, their faces marked with sorrow. Trailing sullenly behind were the three surviving boys from the ill-fated mine-collecting trip. They obviously did not want to be there, but lacked the courage to openly defy the head of the daria.

Philippe Larousse gave her a respectful nod, then turned to Alpha Force. 'Do you have the footage?' he asked.

Hex retrieved the DV tape cassette from his palmtop pouch and Alex pulled the camcorder case from his quad trailer. Philippe took the tape and the case, then walked back into the mud-brick hospital building, with the head of the daria at his side and the sad little group of Sahawaris following behind.

'What do we do now?' asked Amber.

'We wait,' said Hex with just a hint of impatience. He could have sent the footage from the minefield almost as soon as he had filmed it – the digital camcorder had fire-wire technology which allowed him to download the images on to his palmtop and then send them to every major news station in the world – but Philippe had insisted that the boys' parents must be the first to see the footage. Only when the parents gave their permission could it be shown to the rest of the world.

Alpha Force waited silently in the square, watching the closed hospital doors and imagining what the parents of the boys must be going through. Hex busied himself connecting his palmtop to the Net and retrieving his file of the unlisted e-mail addresses of most of the top news programme editors. He smiled as he scanned the list. That had been a worthwhile few hours of hacking.

Hex looked up as the hospital doors creaked open. Philippe, the head of the daria and the three boys came out, their faces etched with the horror of what they had just seen. The parents remained inside. Philippe walked over to Hex and handed him the camcorder.

'They say yes,' he said gruffly.

The Sahawaris gathered around Hex as he sent the footage off to the news stations. When he had finished, he closed the lid of the palmtop and looked at the head of the daria. 'That's done,' he said.

She nodded to show she understood, then looked each of them in the eye, finishing with a special smile for Khalid. Khalid proudly straightened his shoulders and stood as tall as he could.

'I thank you,' said the head of the daria, in heavily accented English. 'We thank you.'

Seven

Paulo woke in the musty heat of the tent. He thought he had heard the musical sound of water trickling into a metal bowl, but the tent was silent now. He swallowed dryly, licked his cracked lips and decided that his thirst must have made him dream of water. Lifting his arm to his face, he peered at his watch in the dim light. It was early evening and he had slept the day away. Beside him, Hex and Alex were still deeply asleep on their camp beds.

Paulo closed his eyes and eased over on to his back with a groan. Every muscle in his body was aching fiercely, but his ears were just about back to normal. He could hear children shouting somewhere in the camp, and inside the tent there was the faintest rustle of cloth and the sound of – stifled giggles . . . ?

He opened his eyes. Li was standing over him with a brass bowl suspended above his head. She grinned at him, then tipped the bowl a little further and a shock of water cascaded down on to his face. Paulo sat up with a yell, shaking his head like a dog and sending sprays of water flying from his dark, curly hair. In the other camp beds, Alex and Hex lurched upright with identical yells as Amber doled out the same treatment.

'C'mon sleepy-heads,' she crowed. 'This is your wake-up call. It's time to rock and roll. Meet you at the Monster.'

Paulo, Hex and Alex used what was left of the water

in the jug to wash themselves, then pulled on the freshly laundered gandourah and sirwal that had been laid out at the bottom of their camp beds. Finally, they pulled on their boots, automatically giving them a shake first to dislodge any scorpions.

Amber, Li and Khalid were waiting for them in a vehicle compound, next to the landing strip that served the camp. The strip was where the big-bellied aid agency planes landed, bringing bags of flour, sugar and lentils for the camp dwellers. The food supplies were loaded into the dusty old lorries in the compound and then distributed amongst the darias.

Paulo smiled fondly when he saw the huge, battered vehicle that Amber, Li and Khalid were leaning against. This was what Amber had nicknamed the Monster. It was an old, flat-bed Unimog, with a six-seater, double-crew cab. Paulo had spotted it in the compound when Alpha Force had first flown in on one of the aid agency planes and he had instantly fallen in love with it. Alpha Force were planning a few days of camping and dune driving after they had completed their mission and Paulo had decided that the Unimog was just what they needed for their trip. He had pestered John Middleton until he had agreed to hire it for them.

'There she is,' crooned Paulo, hurrying over to the Unimog. 'Isn't she a beauty?'

'If you say so,' said Li, rolling her eyes.

'The ideal desert vehicle,' continued Paulo. 'Look at the ground clearance – we will not get bogged down in soft sand in this. And we can drive over rocks with no worries about cracking the sump.'

'Yeah, right. Sump-cracking. That was number one on my worries list,' said Amber.

'Mine too!' continued Paulo, completely missing the sarcasm. 'And she has been converted to diesel, so she is lighter on fuel. Coil-sprung suspension,' he added, patting one of the Unimog's huge wheels. 'Eight gears, tough transmission. She is the ultimate all-terrain vehicle.'

'Paulo,' sighed Hex, 'we're here to load the thing, not to have sex with it.'

'And if we're planning to leave at dawn, we need to get a move on,' added Alex.

'Sorry,' grinned Paulo. 'Let us load.'

Three hours later they had just about finished. Two quads were in place and secure on the Unimog's flat bed, their tents and camping equipment were stored on the rack above the cab and jerry cans of fuel were stacked in the space behind it. The sides of the flat bed were hung with sand ladders, shovels and ten goatskin girbas, each full of water. The girbas were shaped like fat bananas, and they were hung by the cord that tied the two ends closed. This was the traditional way of carrying water in the desert. Water evaporated through the goatskin, acting as a cooling device to stop the water inside heating up.

'Is it going to cope with this load?' asked Hex, eyeing the battered Unimog doubtfully.

'Of course she will,' insisted Paulo. 'Let me tell you about her engine—'

'No, please,' begged Li, clapping her hands over her ears. 'I can't take any more!'

Paulo folded his arms and grinned at her, then his grin faded as he spotted an open-topped jeep speeding towards them across the compound. The front-seat passenger in the jeep was Amber's uncle, and his expression was grim.

'What? What's wrong?' demanded Amber, as the jeep pulled up.

'Bad news,' said John Middleton. 'We've been monitoring all the news channels and, well . . .'

'Well what?'

'Nobody's picked up on the footage.'

'Nobody?' asked Hex, after a shocked silence.

'Not one lousy news agency,' sighed John Middleton. 'I guess the guys here at the camp are right when they say they're a forgotten crisis. The rest of the world doesn't want to know.'

'They are moving,' called the jeep driver, pointing over to the transport plane that was taxiing across to the far end of the landing strip.

'Gotta go,' said John Middleton, heading back to the jeep. 'That's the last plane out tonight, and I'm hitching a lift.'

'Where are you going?'

'To kick a few media asses. I have my contacts – and I've told the guys here that I'll do my best to get that footage shown.'

'What shall we do?' asked Amber.

'You go have your break. You deserve it.'

'But shouldn't we stay in the camp? Show our support?'

'I think we've enjoyed their hospitality for long enough,' said Alex.

The others nodded, knowing exactly what he meant. Sahawari hospitality was legendary, even in the refugee camp where everything was in short supply. Someone always kept the water jugs in their tents topped up, while the rest of the camp operated a system of rationing. There was no natural water supply there – a steady stream of tankers had to ferry water in to keep the cisterns full. Food was in short supply too. The aid agencies could only supply the basics and the Sahawaris supplemented this by keeping little herds of sheep, goats and camels on the edges of the camp. They had even managed the small miracle of creating vegetable gardens in the middle of the desert. These extras helped, but there was still not enough food to go round and Alpha Force had become increasingly uncomfortable with having plates full of vegetables and meat presented to them at every meal.

'Alex is right,' agreed John Middleton. 'It's time to leave. You go and enjoy your dune driving. I want you to listen to Khalid, though. He knows the safe areas and the places to avoid. Right, Khalid?'

Khalid nodded solemnly. He was acting as their guide on the trip and he took the responsibility very seriously. Parts of Algeria were very dangerous to foreigners. Some routes were plagued by bandits and there were fundamentalist groups operating in the north of the country that would not think twice about killing a group of westerners.

'Is safe, where we go,' said Khalid. 'I promise.'

'Good lad,' smiled John Middleton. He kissed Amber goodbye and nodded to the rest of them. 'Keep in touch,' he said, pointing to the pouch where Hex kept his palmtop.

He gave a thumbs-up sign and climbed into the jeep. 'Oh, I nearly forgot,' he said, rummaging through his briefcase and pulling out a slim black box. 'Since I'm not going to be around for a few days, you need to hand this

43

tracker unit over to Philippe before you set off on your trip. That way he can find you if anything goes wrong. You are all wearing your trackers, aren't you?'

'Yes, Uncle,' sighed Amber, reaching up and stuffing the tracker device into the door pocket of the Unimog.

'Let me see.'

Wordlessly, Alex, Paulo and Hex lifted their shirts and pointed to their belt buckles, while Amber and Li hooked out the lockets they were wearing around their necks. The buckles and the lockets all carried concealed tracker devices within them.

'And you have your insulin? Your blood-sugar testing kit?' continued John Middleton, looking at Amber.

'Uncle! I may be a diabetic, but I'm all growed up. You don't need to keep checking up on me!'

John Middleton merely raised his eyebrows and waited.

'It's all in here,' sighed Amber, pointing to the pouch at her belt. 'Wanna make sure my hands are clean, too?' she added sweetly.

'OK,' grinned John Middleton. 'I'll get out of your hair.'

'Let's go see what's happening in the square,' said Amber, once they had waved the plane off. 'You coming, Khalid?'

Khalid hesitated. 'No, I stay here,' he said, gesturing to the loaded Unimog. 'I sleep here. Under. I guard.'

'It'll be safe here, Khalid,' said Alex.

Khalid shrugged. 'I stay.'

'You're just scared we might leave you behind,' teased Li and Khalid gave her a broad smile.

'Do you think he'll be OK out here on his own?' asked

Amber as Alpha Force headed away towards the centre of the daria.

'He won't be on his own,' said Hex as a tiny girl with a gap-toothed smile scurried into the compound and headed straight for Khalid. 'He'll have the munchkin for company.'

The others laughed and gave Khalid a casual wave before heading off into the camp. If they had known what was going to happen in the deserted compound that night, they would not have left his side.

Eight

'There's no sign of life,' said Alex as they strolled back to the compound at dawn the next morning. 'I would've thought he'd be up and raring to go by now.'

'Khalid slept in!' crowed Amber. 'All that garbage about "I rise with the sun, always," and he's still snoring under the truck. What a fraud! Come on, you guys, let's sneak up on him.'

'He might not be there,' said Paulo. 'Maybe he has gone to get some breakfast.'

'No.' Li shook her head. 'He wouldn't risk leaving the Unimog even for a minute in case we left without him.'

'That's true,' said Hex. 'He wouldn't.' He came to a halt and frowned at the dark bulk of the Unimog. 'Something's wrong,' he said flatly.

The others stopped too and looked at one another uneasily. When Hex had a bad feeling about a situation, he was usually proved right and they had heard enough tales about bandits and fundamentalist groups to put them instantly on their guard. A loud, metallic crash made them all jump. It was coming from the far side of the Unimog.

'Split up,' whispered Alex, and Alpha Force melted away into the early dawn light. Paulo and Li dodged to the right, behind a stack of pallets, while Amber, Hex and Alex headed left, using a line of lorries for cover.

The metallic crash came again and they all instinctively ducked to the ground. Seconds later they were up again, slipping between the rows of vehicles like shadows.

Minutes later, Alex, Amber and Hex flattened themselves against the side of a truck that was parallel with the Unimog. Alex eased round the back of the truck until he had the Unimog in view. It was facing them head on, about ten metres away across the stony, hard-packed ground. The far side of the Unimog was in view, but it was deserted. So what had been making the metallic crash? As he watched, a gust of desert wind blustered across the compound and one of the Unimog's cab doors swung open, slamming against the side of the vehicle. The wind died and the door slowly swung back until it was nearly, but not quite, closed.

Alex felt his heart sink. Khalid would never leave the door slamming against the side of the Unimog like that. Hex was right: there was something wrong. He went into a crouch and peered under the vehicle. He could see no sign of a body lying underneath, but the ground below the vehicle was still full of shadows. Alex eased back up and tried to scan the inside of the cab but the windscreen reflected the low sun back into his eyes. There was only one thing for it. He was going to have to get closer.

Alex waited until he could see that Paulo and Li were in position behind the last truck in the row opposite. He motioned them to stay there, then turned to Amber and Hex. 'I'm going in,' he whispered. 'Hex, watch my back. OK?'

Hex nodded, his green eyes steady and determined, and Alex immediately felt better. Hex might not have much to say on the subject of friendship, but Alex knew he would never abandon a mate.

Alex turned to Amber. 'You're our back-up, Amber. If things turn bad, I want you to get out of here and bring some help.'

'Get help. You got it,' whispered Amber, looking into his eyes with an equal mixture of fear and determination.

Alex nodded to them both, then he took a deep breath and raced across the open ground towards the Unimog at a crouching run. As he reached the swinging cab door, he rolled past it to make himself less of a target, then came to his feet again and flattened himself against the big front wheel of the vehicle. Nothing moved inside the cab, so he reached up and nudged open the door with his hand. Still nothing. Alex clenched his jaw, then made himself turn and look up, expecting to come face to face with the barrel of a Kalashnikov. The cab was empty.

Alex sagged against the wheel with relief and something shot out from under the Unimog and grabbed him around the ankle.

Hex heard Alex yell, then saw him fall. He launched himself forward at the same time as Li broke cover from the opposite direction, closely followed by Paulo. Amber wanted to follow but made herself hang back, ready to go for extra help if it was needed. The other three reached Alex together and Li automatically went into a fighting stance, balanced on the balls of her feet, while Hex lunged under the truck to free Alex's leg. He grabbed hold of something, yanked hard – and a scared little gap-toothed girl slid out from under the Unimog with her hand still gripping Alex's ankle.

'That's the one who's always with Khalid,' said Li, once they had recovered.

'She was here last night,' called Amber, hurrying over. 'She arrived just as we were leaving, remember?'

'Yeah, I remember. The munchkin,' said Hex.

Paulo crouched down and checked that there was no-one else under the Unimog, then he turned to look at the little girl. Her face was smeared with dust and tears and her eyes were wide with fear. 'Hello,' he said with a gentle smile. 'Are you hurt?'

The little girl choked back a sob and stared at him uncomprehendingly.

'She doesn't speak English,' said Amber.

Paulo tried again. 'Can you tell us, where is Khalid?'

At the mention of Khalid, the little girl grabbed on to Paulo's shirt cuff and launched into a torrent of words in her own language. Now it was Paulo's turn not to understand. He shrugged helplessly and looked up at Amber, the language expert of the group.

'I'll try her with French,' said Amber, squatting down beside Paulo. French was the second language of Algeria – a legacy of the time when the country was a colony of France.

Amber began to talk slowly and clearly in French and the little girl's face brightened with understanding. She began to answer Amber's questions, speaking so fast that she was almost gabbling.

'She says she and Khalid were sleeping beside the Unimog, when the men came in the night,' translated Amber. 'The men were driving past, heading north, but they stopped when they saw her and Khalid. Khalid told her to hide under the Unimog.'

'What sort of men?' asked Alex. 'Bandits?'

Amber turned back to the little girl and the others waited impatiently.

'No, not bandits. She says . . . it sounds like she's saying "the child stealers",' said Amber.

The little girl began talking again and Amber listened and translated at the same time.

'They had a Unimog, like this one, but the cab was smaller and the back was covered like an army truck. There were bench seats down the sides and these seats were full of children.'

'But why did they take Khalid?' asked Li.

'She says when the leader found out Khalid had no family, he took him away. Khalid went without a struggle because he did not want the man to find her too.'

'This leader, can she tell us anything about him?' asked Hex.

Amber asked the question and the little girl gave a two-word answer they all understood: *'Le scorpion.'*

'The scorpion? What does she mean?'

The girl bent down and drew a picture in the dust with her finger. The drawing was crude, but there was no mistaking the curving tail with the stinger on the end. The little girl pointed to the sand drawing, then to her arm.

'A tattoo?' asked Hex. 'He had a tattoo of a scorpion?'

The little girl nodded hard. 'Tattoo,' she repeated.

'I think he must be a trafficker. A child slaver,' said Li. 'My parents came across something like this on their last West African expedition. The traffickers take children from the poorer African countries, smuggle them north and sell them. Sometimes they give the parents money, and sometimes they just kidnap the children off the street. Some end up in the carpet industry in Morocco. Others end up as domestic servants in the Arab countries or Europe. Even worse, they're sold into the sex trade.'

'Ask her how long ago,' said Alex, examining the tyre tracks on the packed-earth track that ran alongside the landing strip.

'I'll try, but that might be a bit tricky,' said Amber. 'She's only little and I'm not sure whether she has much idea of time.'

Amber's conversation with the little girl went on for several minutes and involved a lot of pointing at the sky. Finally, Amber nodded and turned back to the others.

'OK. I've been asking her what the sky was like at the time the child-stealers came. She remembers the position of the moon and a couple of the constellations. If she's remembering right, I'm guessing Khalid was taken roughly two hours ago.'

'Two hours,' said Paulo. 'They will not be too far ahead, not in a Unimog.' He patted the side of the Monster. 'She is a good machine. I could catch them.'

Alpha Force looked at one another as the same idea – to go and get Khalid back – formed in all their minds. Amber bent down to the little girl and gently told her not to worry any more. They would sort everything out. The little girl gave a relieved smile and raced off to see what was for breakfast.

'These tracks won't be around for much longer,' said Alex, watching the little girl skip away. 'There'll be other traffic soon – and that wind is getting stronger.'

'What about Philippe?' said Paulo. 'Won't he wonder where we've gone?'

Hex shrugged. 'I don't see why. He knew we were planning to set off at dawn with Khalid. He'll just presume that we've gone off on our trip to the dunes, as planned.'

'The Monster's packed and ready to go,' said Amber. 'Guys? What do you think?'

'Why not?' said Li with a grin, climbing up into the cab. 'Let's go get Khalid.'

Nine

The Monster's engine idled as Paulo stared out through the dusty windscreen at the deep wadi which cut across their path. The Unimog was poised on the edge of the bank that led down into the dry river bed. Paulo had already negotiated the vehicle across several wadis, but none of them had sides as steep as this one.

'Can you do it?' asked Amber.

Paulo looked across at her, then back to the slope. His jaw was clenched so tightly, the muscles were jumping.

'We're out in the middle of nowhere, here,' said Amber. 'If you don't think you can do it, we'll find another way round. It's not worth the risk—'

Amber stopped as Paulo engaged four-wheel drive and put the Unimog into first gear. He touched the accelerator and eased the big vehicle over the edge of the slope. Everyone gasped as it plunged down the bank at such an acute angle it seemed almost vertical.

'Brake! Brake!' yelled Amber as the Unimog's chassis groaned and shook. Instead, Paulo took his foot from the brake pedal and placed it on the floor.

'Are you crazy?' yelled Amber.

'If I brake on a slope like this, I will put her into a skid,' said Paulo, gripping the steering wheel so hard his knuckles were white. 'She is in the lowest gear. I must let her find her own way down.'

Just then, the Unimog began to slide as the wheels lost traction.

'Brake! Now!' demanded Amber, but Paulo did the opposite. He touched the accelerator gently until he felt the speed of the spinning wheels catch up with the speed of the descent. The wheels bit, finding traction again, and he eased back off the throttle.

It worked. The Unimog creaked and groaned its way down to the dry bed of the wadi, then jounced off the slope and on to level ground. Paulo let out a sigh of relief and headed out across the dry river bed. Almost immediately he encountered another problem as the Unimog drove into a drift of soft sand that had gathered in the wadi. The engine roared as the wheels lost traction again. Quickly, Paulo accelerated to keep the momentum going. If the Monster slowed too much, they would become bogged down and they could not afford any delays.

'Come on,' he muttered fiercely. 'Come on!'

The Monster wallowed for a few seconds, then the combination of low gear and four-wheel drive triumphed and the big wheels found enough traction to break free of the soft sand on to firmer ground. It lurched forward with a jerk and they all jolted back in their seats.

'Watch it, Paulo!' yelled Hex from one of the back seats. He held up his palmtop. 'I'm talking to my friends here! I've hit so many wrong keys, they're going to think I'm an idiot.'

'Yeah, well, it's about time they found out the truth,' snapped Amber, turning from her seat in the front to glare at Hex. 'Paulo's doing his best,' she added, forgetting that she had been calling him crazy just a minute earlier. 'Right, Paulo?'

Paulo said nothing, but as he stared at the far bank of the wadi, trying to pick the best route back out, his face was stony. A tense silence descended in the cab of the Unimog. They were all getting edgy. Alpha Force had been pursuing the slavers for ten hours and it had been tough going.

Alex was in the front of the cab. He was their tracker, following the tyre tracks of the other Unimog across the desert while Paulo concentrated on the driving. The trouble was, the tracks had become progressively harder to follow as the day went on. To start with, they had been driving across the type of desert known as reg: vast plains of silty gravel and stones that had been deposited over ten million years earlier when the Sahara was mainly sea. The tyre tracks were easy to follow in the reg, standing out clearly in the silt as two darker lines stretching towards the horizon, but then they had disappeared into a great field of boulders. Paulo had slowed to a crawl to negotiate the boulders, but even so Alex still had to keep clambering down from the cab to scout around for the tracks in the blazing sun. At midday the boulders gave way to a stretch of completely smooth saltpan. By that time the sun was a ball of white fire directly above them, which meant there were no shadows: what little impression the tyres had made on the saltpan was virtually invisible. Alex's eyes were burning with the strain of peering through the glare by the time they reached the other side of the saltpan.

Hex had spent the hours crouched over his palmtop in the back of the cab, weaving together all the fine threads of information he could find on the child slave trade, and in particular the Scorpion. Slowly, using all his far-flung contacts, he had built up a picture of a shadowy individual who had been operating for years, making regular trafficking runs from Nigeria, Benin or the Ivory Coast, up through the Sahara to Morocco. The authorities and the child protection agencies knew about him, but they had never managed to catch him. He was very good at staying invisible, with a knack for knowing who to bribe, who to threaten and even, if the rumours were correct, who to kill.

'Keep away from the Scorpion,' warned one of Hex's Nigerian contacts. 'This man is very bad news.' Hex scowled when he saw that message on the palmtop's little screen. He was beginning to wonder whether Alpha Force had taken on more than they could manage this time.

Amber sat between Alex and Paulo, navigating with the GPS unit. As well as recording their route and inputting waymarks so that they would be able to find their way back again, she was using the information stored in her unit's worldwide map database to try to work out where the Scorpion was heading. He was going north, that was for sure. Her guess was that he was heading for a small town on the western tip of the Algeria-Morocco border. He was keeping his head down, travelling off-road and staying well away from any of the trans-Saharan highways. In one way this was good – there were bandits operating on the highways and the routes were patrolled by military convoys – but it also meant that they were heading into one of the more remote parts of the Algerian Sahara, and that made Amber nervous. She could map-read and calculate co-ordinates with the best of them, and the GPS unit would pinpoint any location in the desert to within fifty metres, but all that counted for nothing if they were involved in an accident. It was useless knowing exactly where you were, if you were trapped in an overturned Unimog with nothing but sand for miles around. To make things worse, she had discovered the tracker unit she was supposed to have given to Philippe still wedged in the door pocket where she had shoved it the night before. That meant their only contact with the outside world was via Hex's palmtop.

Li was doing nothing at all. She was a passenger and it was driving her crazy. Everyone else had a job to do, while she slouched in the back of the Unimog feeling very much like a spare part. She was still ashamed of her behaviour at the minefield. She had put Hex and Paulo in danger because of her own stupidity and now all she wanted to do was prove to the rest of Alpha Force how useful she could be. But so far they seemed to be managing fine without her. Li scowled and slumped further down in her seat.

Paulo set the Unimog up the slope that would take them out of the wadi. The big engine did not let him down, and minutes later he was easing the front wheels on to the level ground at the top of the bank. He let out a deep breath and rolled his shoulders to try to ease the tension. That had been the most difficult bit of driving so far, and the terrain had not been easy.

Alex squinted through the fierce glare of the sun as he looked for the tyre tracks they were following. 'Over there,' he said, pointing the way for Paulo, and they headed on in silence, moving further and further north across a stretch of level ground towards a long line of dunes.

The Scorpion's Unimog was still nowhere in sight half an hour later, when they had reached the beginnings of the dune system. Alex rubbed his eyes tiredly, then sat up in his seat as he spotted the tyre tracks swinging over to the left. 'They're turning,' he said, pointing the way for Paulo.

Paulo nodded but, instead of turning left to follow the tracks, he brought the Monster to a gentle stop and turned off the engine.

'What?' said Amber, waking from a fitful doze. 'What's happening? Why have we stopped?'

'I was wrong,' admitted Paulo. 'I thought I could catch them. I cannot. We are averaging forty kilometres an hour, no more. If I keep following in their tracks, we may never catch them.'

'What's the alternative?' asked Hex, leaning forward in his seat.

Paulo turned to look at Amber. 'You say they are heading north, always north?'

'Yeah. Straight as an arrow.'

'Straight as an arrow, all this way. So why have they turned now?'

'Ah,' said Alex, realizing what Paulo was getting at. 'They're going round the dunes.'

Li sat up, suddenly catching on. 'So. If we go across the dunes instead of all the way round, we might just catch up with them.'

Amber was working intently on the GPS system, bringing up a 3D map of the area, including the dune system. 'OK. This could work,' she said, holding out the screen for the others. 'That's the dune system. See? There are two things in our favour. The shape is long but very narrow so we could scoot across while they're still working their way around the edge.'

'And the other thing in our favour?' asked Alex.

'Going by this map, the dunes are all reasonably low. That's good from a driving point of view. Right, Paulo?'

'Yes, but there must be a reason why the slavers have chosen to make a diversion,' said Paulo. 'I think they have driven this route many times before. They know the problems. It will be difficult driving. It could be dangerous. We must decide together.'

Li looked around the group, unable to keep the excitement out of her eyes. 'All those in favour of going over the top, raise your hand!' She stuck her hand straight up in the air. Alex followed her lead, then Amber. Hex hesitated, looking at Paulo then raised his hand too.

Paulo nodded, then turned the ignition key. The Monster roared into life. He patted her dashboard, then turned her nose towards the dunes and moved off.

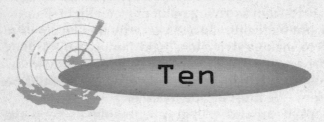

Ten

As the Monster fought her way across the spine of the dune system the rest of Alpha Force saw how good a driver Paulo was. Time after time, he took the Unimog up vast slopes, moving diagonally across the incline at just the right speed to avoid bogging down in the soft sand. Time after time, he clambered down from the cab and climbed the next dune-face to see what was on the other side and plan his next move. He kept to the firmer sand of the windward slopes where he could, riding high on the side of the dune banks so that he had a downward slope for extra momentum if he needed it. It was exhausting work but Paulo stuck at it until, finally, they came to a dune-face so steep, he knew he would have to take it head-on. If he tried to traverse that incline diagonally, the Unimog would roll.

Paulo sighed and prepared to clamber down from the cab once more and check out the other side of the dune.

'I'll come with you,' said Alex, grabbing his binoculars and clambering from the other side of the cab. Instantly, he felt the skin on his face and hands tighten as the sweat evaporated away in the hot wind. The sun hit the back of his neck like a hammer, and under his gandourah and sirwal the sweat formed in a slick layer. Alex licked his dry lips and reminded himself that they were all due a water break when he got back to the Unimog.

They reached the top of the dune and Paulo's exhausted face creased into a tired smile. Ahead of them stretched a sandy plain of low, undulating rises. '*Dios,*' he breathed. 'I thought we would never reach the other side.'

Alex grinned at Paulo, then peered more closely at the plain ahead of them. There was a cluster of low buildings about halfway across. Alex lifted his binoculars and focused.

'It's a village,' he said. 'Out here in the middle of nowhere. There's a small date palmery around an oasis – and some tatty-looking mud-brick houses. A few goats on the outskirts, the usual thing.' He held the binoculars out to Paulo. 'It's a poor place, not much to look at, but they might be able to tell us something about the slavers.'

Paulo ignored the binoculars. He was gazing intently over to the west. 'We may not need to ask,' he said quietly.

Alex turned to look and saw a fast-moving cloud of dust heading towards the village. Quickly, he focused the binoculars on the dust cloud and got his first look at the Scorpion's Unimog. It was rattling along and the canvas covering over the back was rippling in the wind. The canvas was laced tightly shut to hide what was inside. Alex clenched his jaw as he imagined Khalid under that canvas, packed in with a scared huddle of other children, baking in the airless heat and hanging on to the bench seat to stop himself being flung to the floor.

'They're definitely heading for the village,' he said, lowering the binoculars. 'They must be planning a stop.'

He scanned the open ground at the base of the dune. 'See that wadi?'

Paulo gazed down at the dry river bed and nodded.

'Here's what I think we should do,' said Alex. 'We'll hide the Unimog in the wadi, then me and Amber can take one of the quads and head for the village.'

'Why Amber?' asked Paulo.

'She speaks excellent French: if we're spotted, we may need to do some fast talking,' said Alex, gazing across the plain. 'I'm hoping we can sneak in, though. If we take a quad, we can use those bumps and rises for cover.'

'And once you are there?'

'We'll just check things out. See if we can spot Khalid. Find out how much manpower the Scorpion has. Then we'll report back here.'

Alex grinned across at Paulo and slapped him on the shoulder. 'Well done, Paulo! We caught up with them! You did it.'

'Not quite,' said Paulo, looking back at the steep slope they had just climbed. 'I still have to get us over this thing.'

Ten minutes later they were back in the Unimog. 'OK, everyone,' cried Paulo, over the noise of the revving engine. 'Are we ready?'

Alex and Amber braced their feet against the front of the cab, while Hex and Li gripped the armrests of their seats. Paulo had explained what he was going to do. He was planning to push the Monster around the bowl of the dune like a rider on the wall of death, until he had built up enough speed. Then he was going to drive straight at the incline and hope for the best. They only had one chance. If the Unimog lost momentum and slid down into the soft sand at the bottom of the dune bowl, there would be no way of getting out again.

'Go for it!' yelled Li, and Paulo floored the accelerator.

The Monster roared forward, sending up huge gouts of sand from the wheels. The cab leaned further and further over to the side as Paulo circled the bowl, building up speed. The Unimog rose higher and higher up the sides of the bowl and a cyclone of sand and dust whirled outside the cab. Alpha Force hung on, feeling as though their bones were being shaken loose inside them.

'Here we go!' yelled Paulo, twisting the wheel. The Unimog roared as he pointed its nose straight up the slope and Alpha Force were slammed back into their seats. They held their breath as the big machine tackled the incline, straining to climb higher and higher.

'Come on!' yelled Paulo. 'Come on!'

And suddenly they were all yelling at the tops of their voices. 'Come on!' They strained forward in their seats as though that might help the struggling engine. Slowly, the windscreen of the Unimog filled with sky and Paulo watched, trying to judge the right moment to take his foot from the accelerator. It had to be just as the front wheels of the vehicle rolled over the edge of the dune crest. If he eased off too soon, the Unimog might end up straddling the crest on its belly or, even worse, rolling back down into the bottom of the dune bowl. He timed it just right, easing off as the front wheels tipped and allowing the momentum to carry them over the crest, then he slipped into first to take them down the far slope.

Two minutes later they were neatly parked in the

wadi at the base of the dune, out of sight of the village. Paulo leaned back in his seat and closed his eyes.

'That was extreme,' he sighed with a satisfied smile.

In the end it was Alex, Amber and Li who set off to recce the village. Alex had explained to Li that if she came too, they would have to take both quads, which lessened their chances of coming up on the village unobserved, but Li stubbornly refused to stay with the Unimog.

'I'm coming with you,' she insisted. 'I've been sitting in the Monster doing sweet nothing all day.'

They took a twisting route, always keeping higher ground between them and the village. When they came to the last shallow rise before the settlement started, they left the quads hidden at the bottom of the rise and commando-crawled up the slope. Just before they reached the top, Alex signalled to Amber and Li to stay down while he checked things out. He was pretty sure they had not been heard or spotted, but there was no harm in being careful. Cautiously, he lifted his head above the top of the rise, then immediately ducked down again.

'Bingo,' he whispered.

Alex eased the binoculars up until they were resting on the top of the rise, then he peered through them as Amber and Li crawled up on each side of him. Directly ahead of them the slavers' Unimog was parked on the edge of the village. Eight children were hunkered down in a row on the desert side of the vehicle, out of sight of the village. One of the children was Khalid. Alex had picked him out immediately, even without the binoculars. Khalid's Arab looks and clean gandourah made him stand out from the others, who were all West Africans, dressed in crumpled, filthy clothes. There were both girls and boys, most aged between eight and twelve, Alex estimated, although one little girl looked as young as five.

'Nigerians, I think,' whispered Li, gazing at the bedraggled group. 'Maybe Ivory Coast. They've travelled a long way.'

There were two men guarding the children, and a tall, rangy dog with yellow eyes was lying in the shade under the truck with its tongue lolling from its mouth. One of the men turned to lift a girba from the side of the Unimog and Alex groaned as he saw the Kalashnikov slung across the man's back.

'Bad news,' he muttered. 'They're armed.'

The man opened the top of the goatskin girba and poured some of the water into his mouth while the children watched thirstily. Then he poured water for the other guard. The dog scrabbled out from under the truck, wagging its tail eagerly and the man poured a stream of water into the creature's open mouth. Much of the water splashed into the sand in front of the children. The little girl next to Khalid began to cry with thirst and he put a comforting arm around her shoulders. Finally, the guard turned and casually ran the upturned girba along the row of children. Quickly, they held out their cupped hands to catch their share of the sparkling stream of water, then they drank thirstily and licked their palms, catching every last drop.

'Oh, this is evil!' fumed Li. 'We have to do something!'

'It's not going to be that easy,' muttered Alex as he spotted the second guard's Kalashnikov propped against the wheel of the Unimog.

'Where's the Scorpion?' asked Amber, her sharp eyes

noting that neither of the men at the Unimog had a scorpion tattoo on his arm.

'Good question,' said Alex.

He panned the binoculars in a slow arc, trying to spot the leader of the traffickers. The village behind the Unimog was nothing more than a ramshackle cluster of mud-brick houses that had seen better days. Many of them were derelict and abandoned. The houses were built so close together that the narrow, winding alleys between them were like dark tunnels. The oasis on the edge of the village was plainly failing after the years of drought in the Sahara. The network of irrigation ditches was dry and crumbling. There was still an inner ring of date palms growing around the well, but the skeletal remains of a much bigger palmery formed a sombre outer ring. There was a sandy square with a few mange-ridden camels gathered around a rusty water tank, and that was it.

As Alex studied the village, he saw a flurry of movement in the doorway of one of the houses. A tall, good-looking Arab man emerged from the house. He was wearing a layered headcloth to protect his head and neck from the sun, but that was his only concession to desert clothing. The rest of his outfit was right out of a bad Western. His cowboy boots were highly polished, his jeans were skin-tight and the sleeves of his checked shirt were rolled up to the elbow.

'Got him,' grunted Alex as he spotted the scorpion tattoo on the man's left forearm. The Scorpion strolled towards the Unimog and Alex checked him for weapons. He was not carrying a gun or a rifle, but a large knife in a tooled leather sheath hung from his belt.

Two boys followed the Scorpion from the house. The

older one, a boy of about ten, held his head high and did not look back as he walked away. He was holding the hand of a younger boy. His little brother was crying and dragging his feet, looking back at the woman who stood in the doorway with tears streaming down her face. She held out her arms towards him and looked as though she was about to run after him, but a gaunt man appeared behind her, laid a gentle hand on her shoulder and drew her back into the little house.

'We have to do something!' said Li, her face tight with misery as she watched the boys walk away from their home.

Alex shifted uncomfortably. The truth was, none of them had thought this through properly before racing off into the desert after Khalid. 'I'm not sure what we *can* do,' he admitted. 'There's no way we can take on three men with Kalashnikovs. Even if we wait until dark and try to creep up on them, that dog is going to raise the alarm.'

'Couldn't we put the mutt out of action?' asked Amber.

'Then what?' asked Alex. 'We can't just grab Khalid and leave the rest of the kids behind. But we can't take them, either. We don't have the room. And what if one of those kids gets hurt – even killed – because of us. No, I think we must . . .' Alex hesitated, reluctant to admit defeat.

'What?' asked Li.

'I think we must hand this over to the authorities. Hex can send a message on his palmtop, giving them all the details—'

'No,' said Li flatly.

'No?' asked Alex. 'What do you mean, no?'

'I'm not leaving Khalid,' said Li. 'He stayed for me, back at the minefield. He risked being arrested by those Moroccan soldiers. So I'm not leaving him now.'

'Oh, yeah?' mocked Amber. 'So what are you gonna do?'

Li stared defiantly at Alex and Amber. All the shame and fear and frustration of the last few days was beginning to eat away at her and she knew she just had to do something to help Khalid. She had to take action. But what?

'I suppose you could just walk right up to them and ask nicely,' continued Amber sarcastically. 'The nice men might give Khalid back to you . . .' She tailed off as a slow smile spread across Li's face.

'Good idea,' said Li, scrambling down to the quads.

'What's a good idea?' demanded Alex, sliding down after her.

'Walking right up to them,' said Li, rummaging in the box that was strapped to the back of her quad.

'Li, you can't—'

'Maybe *I* couldn't,' said Li, finding the first aid kit and yanking out a length of wide, crepe bandage. 'But Liang could. Look away, Alex.'

Alex frowned. 'Why?'

For answer, Li lifted her shirt up over her head. Alex gaped, then spun round so fast, he nearly tripped over his own feet.

'Listen to me,' he said over his shoulder. 'Whatever you're planning, it's not a good idea. I think we should just head back to the others—'

'OK. You can turn round now.'

Alex stared at Li. She looked like a boy. Her slight figure had been flattened by the thick crepe bandage that was wrapped tightly around her chest under the shirt, and she had twisted her long, silky black hair into a tight knot under her headcloth so that not a single wisp was showing.

'Li—'

'I'm not Li. I'm Liang. I came here from China with my father. He was a foreign oil worker, a labourer. He died in an accident at work and I've been left on my own. I need to find work – an apprenticeship maybe. I speak Chinese and French. I'm strong and I'm a hard worker—'

'OK, I get the picture,' snapped Alex. 'You're planning to walk out there and let yourself be taken by a bunch of armed slave traders. That's very bright. Don't you realize yet how dangerous these men are? It was you who was telling us how they sell the girls into the sex industry!'

'That's why I'm going in as a boy. I'm less at risk that way.'

Alex made a disgusted noise and turned away from her.

'Listen to me, Alex,' said Li, hooking the tracker locket out from under her shirt, 'and you'll see it's not such a bad idea. I'm wearing my tracker. You've got the tracker unit. Once I'm in that truck, I can lead you straight to their base! Then you can call in the authorities and they can mop up the Scorpion and his whole organization in one operation.' She dropped the locket back into her shirt, tucking it under the bandage to keep it hidden.

'You know,' said Amber softly, 'it really isn't such a bad idea.'

Li grinned at Amber and handed over her watch and

the little opal ring she always wore. 'Keep these safe until I can be a girl again,' she said.

Amber took the jewellery, then gave Li a hug. 'Be careful.'

Li nodded. 'I'm going to work my way over to the oasis first. Then it'll look as though I've just walked out of the village.'

'Good idea,' said Amber. 'We'll stay to make sure they take you on board, then we'll head back to the Unimog. We'll be right behind you with that tracker.'

'Wait! Wait a minute,' said Alex. He was floundering. Events were moving rapidly out of his control and he could not seem to get a grip on the situation. 'You haven't even got a weapon—'

'I can look after myself,' smiled Li, adopting a fighting stance. 'Paulo can vouch for that.'

Alex grinned despite himself, remembering how Paulo had once tried to make a move on Li. He had only tried once. Li had thrown him clear over her shoulder.

'OK,' he said, raising his hands in defeat. 'I give in.'

Li's smile widened and her uptilted eyes sparkled at the thought of getting into some action at last. She turned and headed off towards the oasis, keeping low and moving at a steady trot. Amber and Alex watched her go until she slipped out of sight, then they crawled to the top of the rise again and waited for her to walk out of the oasis.

'She'll be fine,' said Amber, noticing Alex's worried face.

'I hope so,' muttered Alex, watching as the Scorpion and his men roughly bundled the two young brothers into the back of the Unimog. 'Because if she isn't, I'll never forgive myself for letting her go.'

Eleven

Li hurried out from the oasis, calling and waving to the traffickers in broken French, her face a picture of anxiety in case they left without her.

'She's good,' breathed Amber admiringly, peering over the top of the rise. 'She even runs like a boy.'

Alex tensed as the man with the Kalashnikov slung across his back spotted Li and reached for his weapon, but the Scorpion put out a hand to stop him. As Alex and Amber watched, Li stood in front of the Scorpion and pleaded with him to take her along too and find her a good apprenticeship. The Scorpion listened, arms folded across his chest, then turned to his men with an amused look on his face. They grinned back. It was not often a boy walked right into their clutches without a struggle.

Turning back to Li, the Scorpion made a show of reluctance. He reached out to test the muscles in her wiry arms, then pulled down her chin to check her teeth. Finally he shrugged and pulled open the canvas flap at the back of the Unimog. Li boosted herself up on the tailgate and disappeared inside the vehicle. The dog jumped in after her, the three men climbed into the cab and the Unimog trundled away, heading north.

'Right,' said Alex. 'Let's move it. We need to get back to the Monster and hit the road double quick. That tracker unit only has a five-kilometre range so we need to catch up and then keep on their tail. It took us twenty minutes to get here on the quads, but we should do the return trip in half that time because we can move straight and fast—'

'What's that?' interrupted Amber, pointing south.

Alex turned to look. The whole of the southern horizon was lost behind a thick, red wall of dust. Within the wall, the dust was constantly moving, swirling in the hot, strengthening wind and rising into the sky in tall spiralling columns.

It was a sandstorm and it was heading their way.

Alex and Amber raced for the quads, pausing only to grab black ski goggles and thin pigskin gloves from the panniers on the back of the machines. They pulled the ski goggles down over their eyes, jammed the gloves on to their hands, then revved the quad engines and blasted out into the desert, standing astride their machines to ride the uneven ground.

They were moving fast, but the sandstorm was faster. Within five minutes it was upon them, and suddenly they were lost in a red, twilight world with only a few metres of visibility. Particles of sand as sharp as pins blasted through every gap in their clothing and the wind that drove into their faces was thick with dust.

It was impossible to breathe. Coughing and choking, they brought the quads to a stop and turned their backs to the wind. The ski goggles kept out the worst of the dust, but still their eyes were streaming. The howling wind made talk pointless, so Alex leaned close to Amber and pointed back to the village.

Amber nodded, understanding. They had to find shelter quickly. She brushed the red dust from the GPS unit strapped to her quad handlebars and peered down at the little screen. She had already waymarked the village on her unit and now she was hoping the system would keep them on track as they struggled to make their way back. Otherwise they might pass within ten metres of the little settlement without even realizing they had missed it.

They were only five minutes out from the village but it took an age to retrace their tracks through the swirling sand. The visibility was so bad, they could only move at a crawl and Amber had to keep stopping to wipe clean the screen of her GPS unit. She was peering at the screen and beginning to think they had overshot despite the navigation system, when Alex reached out and thumped her hard on the shoulder. Startled, Amber looked up and slammed her foot on the brake as a building loomed out of the dust right in front of her.

It was one of the derelict houses on the outskirts of the village. One of the two rooms was open to the desert where the corner of the mud-brick wall had crumbled away. Alex and Amber drove their quads through the hole in the wall and left the machines there, while they staggered through to the shelter of the second room. Alex carried the pannier from the back of his quad bike through with him. He pushed the rotting wooden door shut behind him, then hurried over to the narrow window and closed the shutters.

The sudden drop in the noise level was stunning. For a few seconds they simply stood in the relative quiet and stillness of the dim room, coughing and spluttering and sucking air into their lungs. Then Amber burst into tears.

'What about Li? We were supposed to follow her! She's on her own!'

Alex gritted his teeth. He was worried about Li too. Dread had settled in his chest like a dull pain, but he had to make the best of the situation. He straightened his shoulders and pulled his survival kit from his belt pouch.

'The Scorpion's Unimog won't be going anywhere,' he said reassuringly. 'Nothing can move in this. They'll have to stay put until the storm's over, just like us.'

He fumbled open his survival tin and hooked out his beta-light. He held the little crystal out to Amber and she took it, finding comfort in the pale circle of light emitted by the little crystal. Next Alex searched through the rubble on the floor of the little room until he had found enough pieces of rotting wood to make a fire. He cleared the floor beneath a small gap in the roof that would act as a chimney, then arranged the wood. He always carried dry kindling in his belt pouch and he pulled out a handful now and stuffed it under the wood. Finally he took his flint from the survival tin and struck it until the sparks ignited the kindling. 'There,' he said, as the wood began to catch.

He guided Amber to the fire and sat her down. 'You need food and a hot drink,' he told her. 'You'll feel better after that.'

Amber's sobs subsided into hiccoughs as she busied herself with checking her blood sugar levels. Once she had done that, she took her insulin pen from the pouch and injected herself in the stomach. With a flourish, Alex produced two high-energy bars and a small container of water from the quad pannier. It was important that Amber eat something now, otherwise she could have a hypo attack. If the attack was serious enough, she might pass out, descend into a coma or even die.

As Amber chewed on the energy bar, Alex used his survival tin to heat up some water over the fire. He crumbled in a stock cube and they shared the hot drink in silence, listening to the howling storm outside and wondering what was happening to Li.

Li made eye contact with Khalid as soon as she clambered into the back of the Unimog. His face lit up with incredulous delight, but Li gave him a warning look and shook her head ever so slightly. Khalid was quick on the uptake. He wiped the delighted expression from his face while Li was still blocking the Scorpion's view into the truck. By the time she sat down on the last available bit of bench space, he had replaced it with an expression of dull misery.

The dog jumped in after Li and the Scorpion patted it on the head before glancing around the crowded bench seats, then lacing shut the canvas opening. The inside of the truck was plunged into sudden darkness and Li closed her eyes to help them adjust after the brightness outside. Even though she could see nothing, she was picking up plenty of information about the inside of the Unimog from her other senses, and none of it was good. The heat inside the truck was stifling, the bench she was sitting on was sticky with grease and dirt, and the combined stink of urine and unwashed bodies made her want to retch.

Li opened her eyes and gazed around the dim interior, sizing up her fellow captives and trying to get a feel for who was who in the group. The two boys from the village were sitting opposite her. The younger one was still crying softly and his brother was awkwardly patting his shoulder and staring straight ahead, stony faced. Li guessed he was struggling not to cry too.

'*Bonjour*,' said Li, taking a gamble that the common language for the mixed group in the back of the Unimog was French. '*Je m'appelle Liang.*' They all nodded, seeming to understand her.

'Hakim,' said the older of the village brothers, meeting her eyes with an honest, open gaze. 'And this is Samir.'

Li smiled at Hakim. She liked him immediately and thought she could rely on him as an ally if things turned bad. She turned her attention to the youngest one of the group, a little girl of about five who seemed to have attached herself to Khalid. She was sitting next to him now, clinging on to his arm.

'What's your name?' asked Li.

'Jumoke,' whispered the little girl shyly. 'And this is my friend, Khalid.'

'Jumoke. That's a pretty name.'

The little girl smiled. 'It means Beloved One,' she said without a hint of irony.

Li felt her heart twist. The chances were Jumoke's parents had sold their Beloved One to the Scorpion for a down-payment of ten dollars. 'And where are you from?' she asked, returning Jumoke's smile.

'Nigeria,' said Jumoke.

'Us too,' said the boy sitting next to Li. 'I am Juma and these three are Ajani, Zaid and Rafiki.'

The other three boys nodded but did not speak. Li nodded back to each of them and made a mental note to remember that Juma was the leader of that particular foursome. If she could get Juma on her side, the others would follow.

'I am Kesia,' said one of the two older girls who were sitting together in the far corner of the truck. 'And this is Sisi.'

'We are from Benin,' said Sisi, looking at Li from under her lashes with a coy smile.

Li watched this performance with a puzzled frown until she remembered that, as far as Sisi was concerned, she was a boy called Liang. Li felt a blush spreading across her face and hastily looked away. She met Khalid's amused gaze and raised her eyebrows at him, then casually hooked the locket from her shirt and twisted the chain around her finger. Khalid looked down at the locket, then back to her face, his eyes full of a sudden hope. He knew the locket contained a hidden tracker device and Li could see that he understood exactly why she had made a point of showing it to him.

The Unimog's engine started up, the vehicle lurched forward and Li nearly slid off the bench. Hastily, she shoved the locket back under her shirt and grabbed on to one of the struts supporting the canvas covering. The dog flopped down on to the floor, lying full stretch between the benches and resting its muzzle on its front paws. Li gave the animal a shove to get it off her foot and it rose to its feet again and gave her a yellow-eyed stare. It was a big, lean animal, high in the shoulder, and its long muzzle was on a level with her face as she sat on the bench seat.

Li returned the stare and the dog began a low, rumbling growl in the pit of its belly.

'Don't look it in the eye,' warned Khalid, following her lead and speaking in French. 'It bites if it thinks it's being challenged.'

The growl turned into a snarl and the dog's muzzle

wrinkled back, pulling away from a set of sharp, saliva-coated fangs. Hastily Li looked down at her feet. The dog rumbled for a while longer, then pushed its snout into her neck and sniffed suspiciously. Li held perfectly still, aware that the dog's sharp, curved teeth were centimetres from her jugular vein.

It seemed an age before the dog subsided to the floor again. Li let out her breath and slumped back, trying to ignore the heat and the stink and hoping the rest of Alpha Force were right on her tail.

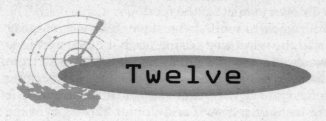

Twelve

While Alex, Li and Amber took the quads to reconnoitre the village, Hex had found a rock in the shade of the dune that gave him a view of the village. He was sitting with his palmtop activated, ready to call for help if things went bad, but he was not expecting any trouble. Alpha Force were all trained in covert surveillance techniques, but Alex was a natural. Keeping out of sight of the slavers would be no problem for him.

Hex focused on the slavers' Unimog once more, but nothing much was happening. He yawned, lowered the binoculars and gazed around the quiet camp. The Monster was parked directly below the towering dune, in the shelter of the wadi. Paulo was sprawled out on the back seats of the cab, deep in an exhausted sleep after his day of extreme driving. A container of water was coming to the boil on the stove that Hex had positioned on a patch of flat ground; five silver-foil packages were lined up beside it.

His stomach gave a loud rumble as he looked down at the boil-in-the bag rations. After a day without food they actually seemed appetizing. He caught the faint note of an engine starting up and turned to look across the plain to the village. He did not need the binoculars to see the Unimog pulling out and heading north in a cloud of dust. The two smaller clouds of dust heading his way must be the quads. Hex grinned, put his palmtop down on the rock next to the binoculars and sprinted down to heat up the food.

As he busied himself at the stove, Hex was vaguely aware that the wind was getting up, but in the lee of the massive shoulder of the dune he was protected from both the sight and the noise of the approaching sandstorm until it was right on top of the camp. The whirling mass of red sand and hot air blasted over the crest of the dune and swirled in from either side in the space of a second. Hex barely had time to jump away from the pot of boiling water as it overturned.

He yelled in shock, but his yell turned into a choking cough as his mouth and throat filled with sand. His eyes felt as though they had been stuck with needles. He closed them tight against the storm, wincing as the sand already trapped under his lids scraped across his corneas. Blind and choking, Hex stumbled in what he thought was the direction of the Unimog until his foot stepped out into thin air and he tumbled down into the stony bottom of the wadi. With a groan he picked himself up again, but he had lost all sense of direction and could not decide which way to go. If he headed the wrong way, he could be staggering along the stony bed of the wadi until he collapsed. As he stood there, hunched against the howling storm and trying to see out of his streaming eyes, a dark shape loomed up beside him.

It was Paulo. He had wrapped his headcloth round and round his face like a bandage and plonked a pair of sunglasses over his eyes. Hex had never been so glad to see the big South American, even if he did look like a cross between a mummy and the invisible man. Hex grabbed Paulo's arm and allowed himself to be guided to the Unimog and up into the shelter of the cab. Once he was in, he collapsed across the front seats, coughing up sand and wiping his streaming eyes as Paulo climbed in after him and pulled the heavy door shut.

It was nearly dark inside the cab. The wind was strong enough to rock the big vehicle on its wheels and the sand hissed and rattled against the metal bodywork, but at least it was possible to breathe again. Hex took several deep, sand-free gasps of air, then sat up and looked across at Paulo.

'Thanks,' he said gratefully over the noise.

'The others?' asked Paulo, unwinding his headcloth.

'Last time I looked, the Scorpion's Unimog was heading north and the quads were heading back this way,' said Hex.

'Into the storm,' said Paulo.

'Yeah, but I'm sure they would've seen it coming and turned back to the village. They'll be sitting this out just like we are.'

Paulo nodded, but his face was worried as he stared out into the storm. 'I wish we could be sure,' he said.

Hex smiled as an idea hit him. 'We can,' he said.

'How?'

'The tracker unit,' said Hex. 'It's in the door pocket next to you.'

Paulo pulled out the slim black box, opened up the lid and extended the telescopic aerial. Hex leaned in as he activated the screen. A grid appeared, with compass bearings and a distance scale in the top corner.

'That's us,' said Hex, pointing to a bright green double blip in the centre of the grid. 'And that's them,' he added, pointing to another green blip over in the north-west quadrant of the screen. 'See? That's exactly where the village is. Told you they'd be holed up there.'

81

'So what is that?' asked Paulo, pointing to a third, smaller blip nearly at the top of the screen, heading north.

Hex frowned, then looked back to the blip in the village. He studied it more closely and realized that it was made up of two flashing green lights, not three.

'Did you say the Scorpion was heading north?' asked Paulo.

The same thought hit them simultaneously. They shared a horrified glance, then turned back to the tracker unit. The single blip was nearly off the screen now.

'The Scorpion's got one of them,' said Hex.

'Which one?' asked Paulo, staring at the single blip. 'And how can they still be moving in this?'

'The storm can't have caught them yet,' said Hex.

The blip reached the edge of the screen and winked out. Paulo thumped the dashboard in frustration. 'Quickly! You must call the authorities and give them the Scorpion's position. Maybe they can head him off from the north.'

Hex nodded and reached for his palmtop, but the pouch under his shirt was empty. A chill ran through him as he remembered that he had left his palmtop on the rock just before the storm hit. 'It's out there,' he said quietly. 'On the rock where I was sitting.'

'*Inferno!*' cursed Paulo. He peered out through the windscreen, trying to judge whether he could make it to the rock without getting lost. He never had the chance. Suddenly the whole vehicle shuddered as something hugely heavy fell on top of them with a massive whump. The cab was plunged into darkness and the noise of the storm stopped in mid-howl as though a switch had been flicked.

'What the hell . . . ?' Hex ducked as the metal roof of the cab groaned, then folded downwards in a V shape above his head. It came to a stop just above the headrest of the middle seat. The windscreen buckled under the pressure with a crack like a starter pistol and the glass splintered into a spider web of fine cracks.

Paulo reached for the door handle and yanked it back, but the door would not budge. Hex tried his door with the same result. They stared at one another and their eyes were wild in the dim, green light from the tracker screen. Neither of them could explain what was happening and that scared them.

'Window,' panted Hex. 'Try the window.'

Paulo grabbed the handle and gave it a powerful wrench just as Hex finally realized what had fallen on to the Unimog.

'No!' yelled Hex, but he was too late. Paulo's window slid halfway down and an avalanche of sand poured into the cab. It filled the floor well and reached their knees with frightening speed. By the time Paulo had managed to force the window almost closed again, the sand was up to their hips.

'*Dios!*' yelled Paulo, holding the tracker unit out of the way of the sand. 'What is happening?'

'It's the dune,' said Hex. 'The base was right up against the side of the wadi. A whole section must've been ready to collapse into it and the storm just pushed it over the edge.'

Paulo swallowed and peered across at Hex in the dim, green light from the tracker screen. 'The dune has fallen into the wadi? Onto us?'

Hex nodded. 'Some of it at least.'

'How much is "some"?' asked Paulo, staring at the solid wall of sand that pressed against the cracked windscreen.

Hex shrugged. 'I don't know,' he said. 'But one thing's for sure. We're buried.'

Thirteen

'I don't understand it.' Amber stared down at her GPS unit, then up at the empty space in front of the dune. 'This is supposed to be accurate to within fifty metres. They should be here. The wadi should be here and they should be parked in it. But there's nothing!'

Alex pulled his headcloth away from his face and stood up on his quad to get a better view. The sun was only just over the horizon and it was difficult to tell the difference between substance and shadow. A muscle jumped in his jaw as he looked around. He could not quite believe what was happening. Li had been taken away in the Scorpion's Unimog while he and Amber had been pinned down all night in a ferocious sandstorm – and now Paulo and Hex had disappeared too. The situation just kept on getting worse.

Alex shook his head, then turned his quad and raced along the edge of the dune base, looking for tyre tracks. He rounded a curve in the side of the dune and a chasm opened up in front of him. With a curse, Alex swung the quad hard to the right, leaning into the turn with all his might. His rear left wheel skidded over the edge of the wadi and the quad started to tip. He found some extra power in the motor and forced the quad away from the edge. He came to a halt well away from the dune and scrambled from the machine.

By the time Amber caught up with him, Alex was standing on the bank at the place where he had nearly lost control of his quad. 'Look at this!' he called to her as she climbed from her machine and hurried over. 'I don't understand it. Here's the wadi at the base of the dune, but it stops dead, right there, as though it ran into a wall.'

'Or the other way round,' said Amber softly, staring wide-eyed at the section of dune they had just skirted.

'What?'

'I think I know where they are, Alex,' said Amber, her voice high with fear.

'Where?' asked Alex.

Amber pointed at the new curve in the dune. 'Under there.'

They raced back to their original position and turned off the quad engines. 'This is it,' said Amber, studying the screen of her GPS unit. 'This is where we left them last night.'

'Listen!' said Alex. 'Did you hear that?'

They both stood stock still, holding their breath. Very faintly, from the slope directly ahead of them, came the sound of a truck horn. They threw themselves at the slope and started digging feverishly, scooping the sand out with their bare hands and sending it arcing back between their legs. The horn sounded again, louder this time, and they threw themselves into the digging with renewed effort.

'Got something,' panted Amber as her hand connected with metal. She brushed the sand away and revealed part of the roof of the Unimog cab. Quickly they found the edge of the roof then cleared the sand away from the side window. It was partly open, but the opening was blocked with sand. Alex knocked the sand away and peered inside. It was still too dark in the cab to see anything but there was no mistaking the sour air that sighed into his face.

'Quick!' he yelled, returning to clearing the sand from the cab door. 'They're out of oxygen!'

They dug until their muscles were screaming, and finally there was enough space to force the door open. Sand poured out of the cab but there was no other movement in the dim interior. Paulo was slumped to one side, clutching the tracker unit to this chest. His face was grey and there was a blue tinge to his lips. Hex was resting against the steering wheel, his head turned towards them. His eyes were closed.

'Are we too late?' quavered Amber.

Just then, Hex's eyelids fluttered open. His green eyes tried to focus, then rolled back in his head. He reached up to the steering wheel and pressed the horn lever. The horn blared out and Hex gave a small nod of satisfaction before his eyes fluttered shut again. He must have been sending this signal in his semi-conscious state for hours.

'We're here, you idiot,' said Amber in a voice choked with tears. 'Enough of the signalling!'

Together, Amber and Alex dragged Paulo and Hex from the cab. Once they were out in the fresh air, the two boys recovered quickly and soon Paulo was sitting up, still clutching the tracker unit and looking around groggily. Hex stumbled to his feet, leaned over and vomited into the sand.

'You took your time,' he gasped, when he could talk again.

'Yeah, well, we would've found you sooner if you hadn't decided to play go seek,' retorted Amber, handing him the container of water from her quad pannier.

Paulo's eyes suddenly became sharp and focused. He looked down at the tracker device, then up to Amber and Alex. 'Li?' he croaked.

'She's with the Scorpion,' said Alex. 'She's under cover, pretending to be a boy called Liang.'

'And you let her go?' said Paulo softly, staring at Alex.

'Yes,' muttered Alex, gazing down at his boots.

Paulo surged to his feet and aimed a punch at Alex's face. His big fist landed squarely enough but he was still too weak to put any power behind it. Alex fell backwards on to the sand with his cheekbone smarting but still intact. He clambered to his feet again but did not retaliate. Part of him felt he had deserved the punch.

'You let her go?' repeated Paulo, staggering as he prepared to punch Alex again.

'Stop it, you big idiot!' yelled Amber, putting herself between Paulo and Alex. 'It's not Alex's fault. You know what Li's like. Once she gets an idea into her head, no-one can stop her.'

For a few seconds Paulo glared at Alex over Amber's shoulder, then the fire left his eyes and he nodded slowly, acknowledging the truth of what she was saying. He stumbled and would have fallen hard if Alex had not caught him. Gently, Alex lowered Paulo to the sand, where he sat with his head down, cradling the tracker unit to his chest.

'She's wearing her tracker device,' said Alex. 'She wanted us to track her to the Scorpion's headquarters, then bring in the authorities.'

'It was a good plan,' mumbled Paulo.

'Still is,' said Hex briskly. 'They must've been caught in the storm too, so they can't be that far ahead, and we know they're heading north. We can catch up with them.'

While Paulo and Hex recovered from their near-suffocation, Alex and Amber dug around the buried Unimog. There was no sign of Hex's palmtop, which meant they had no way of communicating with the outside world, but they did manage to retrieve two jerry cans of fuel and two girbas of water that had not burst under the weight of the sand. The quads' fuel tanks were nearly full and there were bottles of water in the panniers, but they did not know how long they would be following the slavers: they would be no good at all to Li if they ran out of water or fuel in the middle of nowhere.

As well as water bottles, the quad panniers each held a first aid kit, high-energy emergency food rations, a pair of night-vision goggles and two pairs of pigskin gloves and ski goggles. When Paulo and Hex had recovered enough to travel, they all pulled on a pair of the gloves, wrapped the headcloths tightly around their necks and faces and fitted the ski goggles over their eyes. This was essential wear for daytime quad travel through the desert. The strong sun and drying wind meant they had to be completely covered from head to foot to protect against dehydration; even then they would have to stop every hour to drink.

Alex sat astride one quad, with Hex behind him, holding the tracker unit. Paulo took the other quad and Amber clambered on behind. Paulo had rigged some webbing to carry the extra jerry cans of fuel and Hex and Amber each had a girba hanging at their backs.

'Ready?' called Alex, over the revving of the quad engines.

Amber leaned over Paulo's shoulder to make sure the GPS unit on the quad's handlebars was set, then she gave a thumbs-up signal to Alex and thumped Paulo on the shoulder. 'Let's go get Li!' she yelled.

Paulo set a fast pace and the two quads cut through the desert side by side as the sun rose in the sky. They travelled north all through the morning, only stopping for water breaks or for Amber to input waymarks into her GPS unit. Every time they stopped, Paulo looked over at Hex and Hex shook his head. The tracker screen remained depressingly blank and Paulo's face grew more and more grim.

'Are you sure it is working?' he asked at their fifth water halt.

'Yes,' sighed Hex, trying to remain patient. He pointed to the cluster of four green dots in the centre of the screen. 'It's picking up our tracker signals,' he said, looking up at Paulo. 'That means it's working.'

Paulo's shoulders slumped and he turned away, heading back to his quad. Hex turned back to the screen. He became very still, staring intently at the tracker unit. A small green dot had appeared, right at the top of the screen.

'There she is,' he said softly. 'We've found Li.'

Alex took over the lead, responding to Hex's shouted directions. Li's tracker dot was not moving, so the gap was closing quickly when Paulo suddenly pointed ahead and shouted.

'Tracks! I see tyre tracks!'

They brought the quads to a halt and Alex climbed down to study the tracks. 'They're heading north, just as we thought,' he said, straightening up. 'That's their Unimog all right.'

'Are you sure?' asked Amber.

'I followed these tracks for most of yesterday,' said Alex. 'Of course I'm sure.'

'She's still not moving,' said Hex, staring at the screen.

'They must have stopped for food, or something,' said Amber.

'But where?' muttered Paulo, gazing across the stony, flat plain which stretched ahead of them with barely a dip in the ground. 'According to this, she's less than a kilometre away. We should be able to see the Unimog.'

They looked at one another uneasily.

'There's a small rise ahead – look at the rocks over there,' said Amber.

'Yes, but that's not high enough to hide a Unimog,' pointed out Alex.

'It's about a kilometre away,' said Hex, looking from the screen to the rocky rise. 'And it's in the right direction . . .'

'Come on,' said Paulo, running for his quad.

As they drew closer, Paulo shook his head in puzzlement. The rise was little more than a pimple on the face of the plain. Even the quads would have trouble hiding behind it, but the Unimog tracks were heading straight for it. He looked over to Hex to see whether Li's signal had moved on. Hex shook his head and pointed to the rise.

'They definitely stopped here,' said Alex, as the quads pulled up next to the rise. 'See all the footprints around the tyre tracks?' He picked up a discarded jerry can and sniffed at the open top. 'They refuelled, then carried on north,' he finished, pointing out the tracks heading away from the rise.

'So why is Li's tracker signal still here?' asked Hex, staring at the screen.

'Guys?' called Amber. 'Come look at this.'

As they drew closer to Amber, they could all see the dread on her face. Paulo felt a cold hand trace a path all the way down his back as he saw what Amber was holding out to them. It was a small rock. One side of the rock was smeared with blood and hair.

'*Dios*,' he breathed, looking around wildly. A few metres away the sand was churned up, as though there had been a struggle there. Paulo hurried over and stopped, staring down at the ground. A strange track led away from the churned-up area. There was a central rut, with deep holes and gouges in the ground alongside it. On the other side, gouts and splashes of something had spilled on to the ground, forming a sticky, brown crust.

Paulo leaned closer and caught the unmistakable smell of blood. Horrified, he pulled back and looked at the others, suddenly realizing what the odd tracks meant. 'Someone dragged themselves away from here,' he said. 'They were bleeding. Lots of blood.'

They all turned and looked up to where the dragging tracks disappeared over the top of the low rise. Amber swallowed and her throat clicked loudly in the silence.

'Li's signal?' she asked.

Hex held out the tracker unit. The dot marking Li's position was still in the centre of the screen, alongside the other four dots. 'She must be over the rise,' he said.

Alpha Force looked at one another, then started up the slope, following the splashes of blood.

Fourteen

Li struggled to stay awake. Her eyes and throat felt as though they were full of needles and all her muscles ached. She had not slept all night. Less than fifteen minutes after she had left the village in the back of the Scorpion's Unimog, the sandstorm overtook them. Within seconds, visibility was down to a few metres and the big vehicle had shuddered to a halt. The Scorpion had taken his dog into the cab with him, leaving the children to huddle together in the back of the truck.

All night the wind had howled, shaking the truck bed and making the canvas cover yank against the cords that secured it to the base. Sand blasted into the dim interior through every gap and hole in the canvas and soon the air was thick with dust. Pulling their headcloths tightly across their noses, they had formed a huddle on the stinking floor of the truck, with the younger ones in the middle, and waited for the storm to end.

The storm had raged until dawn, by which time they were all exhausted, but the Scorpion had only allowed them a hurried water break before herding them all back into the truck and continuing the journey. They had been driving for hours now. Jumoke was so exhausted she was sleeping with her head against Khalid's chest despite the relentless rocking and jolting in the back of the Unimog. Khalid was supporting her with one arm and holding on to the bench with the other. Samir was asleep too, resting against Hakim, but everyone else was awake, concentrating on clinging on to the benches and trying to ignore their thirst.

Suddenly the engine spluttered and died and the Unimog coasted to a halt. The cab doors slammed and Li could hear the Scorpion shouting at his men outside the truck. She tried to concentrate on what he was saying, but her head was ringing and her tired brain was having trouble understanding. It took her a few seconds to realize he was talking in Arabic.

'What's he saying?' she asked Khalid in French.

'He says they cannot afford any more delays,' replied Khalid. 'He says they must get there tonight. The auction is tomorrow and he has buyers coming from all over Morocco.'

'Auction?' said Juma. 'What do you mean, auction?'

Li sighed. She had decided to keep quiet about their situation until they had reached their destination and Alpha Force had given her some sort of signal. There was no point in distressing the younger ones until she was sure that rescue was at hand. Now it seemed she had no choice. She looked Juma in the eye. 'A slave auction. He is going to sell us, Juma. Sell us as slaves.'

'No!' Juma shook his head fiercely. 'Our fathers told us we would become apprentices and learn a trade.'

The other boys nodded and Juma glared at Li, but she could see that, behind his denials, he knew the truth. He just did not want to admit it.

'We will learn a trade and send money back to our families in Nigeria,' said Juma, folding his arms. 'That was the agreement.'

'We are to be given positions with rich families,' said Sisi.

'And we shall be sent to school in return for a little housework,' added Kesia.

Li looked at the two girls and saw that they too were clinging on to the promises the Scorpion had made to their parents, rather than face up to the truth.

'I shall earn a lot of money in Morocco, braiding hair for the tourists,' said Jumoke, sitting up and rubbing her sore eyes.

Li smiled at the little girl. She didn't have the heart to tell her that she would probably be sold to a street trader, who would take all the money she made.

Li turned to look at Hakim. His face was haggard as he stared at her and his arm tightened around the sleeping Samir. Hakim knew she was telling the truth. He spoke Arabic and he had heard the Scorpion shouting at his men.

'Don't worry, Hakim,' she said. 'I have a plan. When we get to the auction house, we will escape.'

Hakim shook his head. 'I must go back to warn my father now, while my village is still only a day's walk away.'

'It is too risky, Hakim! They have guns – and there is nowhere to hide out there!'

Hakim turned and peered out through a split in the canvas. 'There is a small rise,' he said, turning back to Li. 'If I can get behind it without them seeing me, I can hide there until the truck leaves. But . . .' Hakim hesitated, looking down at his sleeping brother. 'I must leave Samir here. He is too young to make the journey. Will you look after him until I come back with the men from the village?'

'Of course I will. But I don't think you should try it, Hakim!' hissed Li. 'Wait until we get to the auction house. It's too dangerous out here!'

Just then, the canvas flaps at the back of the truck were wrenched open. One of the Scorpion's men flung a half-empty girba into the back of the truck, then pushed Li's legs out of the way and yanked a jerry can of fuel out from under the bench. He started to lace the canvas flaps together again, but a shout from the Scorpion made him jump to carry the jerry can round to the front. He left the last part of the canvas flaps untied.

Li caught Hakim's eye and shook her head, but she could see it was useless. He was determined to go. Wordlessly, Li pulled the plug from the neck of the girba and passed it to him. He took a long drink, then woke Samir and handed him the waterskin. While his brother was occupied with quenching his thirst, Hakim took a deep breath and slipped out under the canvas flaps.

Li crouched on the floor, watching through the little gap in the canvas and willing Hakim on. He landed softly and turned to check that the three slavers were still occupied at the front of the vehicle. Satisfied, he began to sprint away towards the rise, but the dog sprang out from under the truck after him.

Li's heart clenched but she dared not call out in case she alerted the men at the front of the truck. As she watched, Hakim turned to face the dog just as it leaped for him. It knocked him to the ground and stood over him, snarling. Hakim scrabbled in the stony dirt until he found a fist-sized rock. He gripped the rock tightly and swung it at the dog, clubbing it on the side of the head as hard as he could. The dog yelped and fell on to its side, twitching and bleeding.

Hakim staggered to his feet again and turned to run. There was a shout from the front of the truck but he kept going until two shots rang out, hitting the ground a metre ahead of him and blasting clouds of dirt into the air. Hakim stopped and turned, raising his hands. The Scorpion's men grabbed him by the arms and dragged him back to the truck.

The Scorpion was hunched over his dog, which was lying still with its tongue hanging from the side of its mouth. He stroked the animal's bony head and crooned to it, until it opened its eyes and staggered to its feet with a whine. As soon as the Scorpion was sure his dog was not going to die, he rose to his feet and turned to Hakim.

'You could have killed him,' said the Scorpion, switching to French. His voice was hoarse with fury. He back-handed Hakim twice across the face and his signet ring cut the boy's mouth open. Hakim took the blows silently, then stared defiantly at the Scorpion, blood pouring down his chin.

'You want to leave us?' rasped the Scorpion. 'Very well.'

Li gasped as the slaver pulled a wicked-looking, curved knife from the sheath at his belt. He stepped towards Hakim and his men turned the boy to give their boss a clearer target.

Li could not stand by any longer. She launched herself from the truck, landing a flying kick in the throat of the nearest man as she came down. He let go of Hakim, dropped his Kalashnikov and fell to the ground, clutching his windpipe. Li grabbed the weapon and rolled to her feet. Before the second man had time to react, she came up behind him and clubbed him on the back of the neck with the rifle butt.

Hakim took the chance to break free while the second man was still reeling from the blow. The man staggered and leaned on his Kalashnikov while he put a hand up to the back of his neck. Hakim lashed out with his foot and kicked the rifle away. Caught by surprise, the man fell and Hakim scurried to pick up the weapon.

Li grinned when she saw Hakim take possession of the second Kalashnikov. She was beginning to think they might just get out of this situation alive.

'Keep them in your sights!' she yelled, pointing to the two men on the ground. Hakim nodded, raising his Kalashnikov, and Li turned, ready to deal with the Scorpion. She froze, her eyes widening with horror at what she saw.

The Scorpion was standing at the back of the truck, holding a crying Samir in front of him. His curved knife was digging into the side of Samir's throat and a thin trickle of blood was running down the boy's neck.

'Put down the weapons,' said the Scorpion coldly.

Li felt the hope drain out of her. There was no way they could refuse. If they did, Samir would die. She looked over at Hakim. He was already laying the Kalashnikov on the ground, never taking his eyes off his little brother. Li sighed and did the same.

'On your feet,' barked the Scorpion to his men. Coughing and staggering, they picked themselves up, retrieved their weapons and trained them on Li and Hakim. Li narrowed her eyes, judging her chances if she used her fighting skills again, but the element of surprise had gone and the men were standing well back, out of range. Li relaxed and stood balanced, feet apart and arms by her sides, waiting for her next chance. She never got it.

Suddenly the Scorpion pushed Samir to the ground and sprang for Li. His knife flashed in the sun as he lunged for her face. Before she could move, the knife sliced past her ear, close enough for her to hear the swish of the blade. She winced, waiting for the pain to start, but there was nothing. The Scorpion stepped back and Li moved up on to the balls of her feet, to be ready for his next attack. He merely stood there, watching her with a cold smile.

Li was getting seriously freaked. What was he waiting for? His first lunge had missed: why didn't he try again? A chill ran through her as she considered the possibility that the knife had injured her so seriously, she was experiencing no pain. Cautiously, Li raised her hand to her neck, expecting to feel the slick warmth of her own blood. All she found was whole, undamaged skin. She peered down at her hand, double-checking. When she looked up again, the Scorpion was holding something up for her to see. Dangling from his fingers was a twist of her long, silky black hair.

Li froze in shock. The tendril of hair must have come loose from her headcloth during the fight. Quickly, she tucked the rest of the escaped hair back under her headcloth, even though it was too late now. The Scorpion already knew she was a girl. He lunged forward again and, before Li could react, yanked the layered cloth from her head. Her long black hair came tumbling down over her shoulders, falling nearly to her waist. There was a gasp from the Scorpion's men and from the children in the truck, who were all peering through holes and gaps in the canvas.

Still smiling coldly, the Scorpion stepped up to Li and, using the knife, pulled her gandourah open at the neck. He saw the bandage wrapped around her chest and his smile widened.

'Your value has just increased,' he said. 'There will be many men interested in buying you tomorrow. A pretty, light-skinned girl is worth a lot more than a scrawny boy.'

The dog whimpered again from under the shade of the Unimog and the Scorpion's expression hardened. 'Get the others out here,' he ordered his men. 'I want them to see this.'

Once the rest of the children were gathered in a frightened huddle outside the truck, the Scorpion grabbed hold of Samir and pulled him away from his big brother. Hakim looked over at Li, wordlessly reminding her of her promise to look after Samir. She nodded and gathered up the little boy, holding his shaking body in the circle of her arms.

Satisfied, Hakim turned to face the Scorpion. The slaver back-handed him again, hard enough to make him fall to the ground. Then he bent down, grabbed Hakim's right ankle and pulled his leg up into the air. Hakim's baggy sirwal slid down and pooled at his hip, leaving his skinny leg exposed.

'This is what we do to those who try to run away,' said the Scorpion, looking at the other children.

His curved knife flashed again and Hakim gave an agonized scream as the blade cut deep into the back of his leg, just above the knee. It sliced through the two tendons behind the knee and Li heard the snap as they parted from the big muscles at the back of Hakim's thigh. The muscles contracted, shrinking up towards the tendons that anchored them to his hip. The knife had sliced through a major artery and arcs of bright blood began to pump from the back of Hakim's knee on to the Scorpion's western jeans and checked shirt. He grimaced with distaste and stepped back, letting go of Hakim's ankle. Hakim screamed again as his leg flopped to the ground.

'Now, he cannot run,' said the Scorpion, staring at the horrified faces of the other children. 'Remember, you do not need the use of your legs to weave carpets.'

Quickly, Li shepherded Samir over to the group of children and handed him to Khalid, then she walked back towards Hakim, picking up her discarded headcloth on the way. She wanted to bind his leg for him and stop the worst of the bleeding. She wanted to do something, anything, to stop the high screams that were coming from his throat, but the Scorpion's two henchmen stepped in front of her, forcing her to stop.

'Get them back in the truck,' ordered the Scorpion.

The men turned and bent towards Hakim.

'Not him,' said the Scorpion.

'You can't leave him here,' protested Li.

'He hurt my dog!' snarled the Scorpion, his dark eyes flashing with anger again for an instant.

'But you'll lose money,' said Li desperately. 'Don't you want to sell him? Like you said, he could still weave carpets.'

'I won't be able to sell this one,' said the Scorpion, recovering his composure. 'I cut too deep this time. He will bleed to death soon.'

The Scorpion turned his back on Hakim, dismissing him. Quickly Li reached inside her gandourah and pulled out the locket with the tracker device inside. She lifted the chain over her head, then held it clutched in her hand while she checked on the slavers. The Scorpion was squatting with his back to her, stroking his dog; the two henchmen were still hustling the other children into the back of the truck.

Li took two sideways steps, then swiftly bent down and slipped the locket around Hakim's neck. 'My friends are following,' she whispered. 'They will find you.'

Hakim, deep in his pain, gave no sign of having heard her. He was whimpering now, writhing on the ground and clutching at his injured leg. Li gave his shoulder a squeeze and made herself step away. She did not want the men to find the locket and destroy Hakim's only chance of being found. Tears filled her eyes and spilled down her cheeks as she moved towards the truck.

Li clambered into the back to join the others. She sat down next to Samir and put her arm around his shoulders. He was too shocked to cry. He sat rigidly on the bench, shaking all over but making no noise at all. Li held him close as the Unimog started on its way again and she vowed to repay the Scorpion for this if it was the last thing she ever did.

Fifteen

They found the boy just beyond the rise, with Li's tracker locket strung around his neck. He was lying on his back with his head pillowed on his arm and his eyes closed as though he had simply fallen asleep.

'Are you sure?' whispered Amber, staring at the peaceful face. 'Check again, Paulo.'

Paulo pressed his fingers to the boy's neck, feeling for a pulse. He kept his fingers in place for a long time, but there was not even the faintest flicker of life. 'I am sure,' said Paulo finally. 'He is dead. He has been dead for a while.'

'It's the boy from the village,' said Alex. 'The older one of the two brothers.'

'What killed him?' asked Amber.

'There's blood everywhere,' said Hex, staring down at the boy's bloodstained clothes. 'It's hard to tell where it came from.'

Paulo looked over the body, noting that the bloodstains were most concentrated on the right leg of the boy's sirwal. Gently he eased the boy on to his left side and pulled the blood-stiffened material away from the right leg until the gaping wound behind the knee was revealed.

'What the hell happened there?' gasped Hex.

'They had a dog,' said Amber faintly. 'A big, ugly-looking mutt.'

Alex shook his head. 'This isn't a dog attack. The wound is too neat.' He looked down at Paulo, who was still squatting by the body. 'Knife?' he asked.

Paulo nodded. 'I, too, think it was done with a knife.' He leaned forward to inspect the wound more closely, then shook his head. 'The cut severed the hamstring tendons,' he said, looking up at the others.

'Why would someone do that?' asked Amber, in a quavering voice.

'To stop him from running away,' said Hex grimly. 'It's one of the Scorpion's trademarks.'

'He was carrying a knife,' said Alex, remembering the hand-tooled leather sheath he had seen on the Scorpion's belt.

'The cut also severed a major artery,' continued Paulo. 'That is what killed this boy. He bled to death. Li did her best to save him by guiding us here with the tracker, but there was no real chance for him. No chance at all.'

They scraped out a bed for the boy in the hard ground and laid him in it, covering his face with his headcloth. Then they built a low cairn of rocks and stones over him, to mark his position and protect the body from scavengers. They left the tracker device around his neck, so that he could be found later and given a proper funeral.

'Someone should say something,' said Amber as they stood around the finished cairn.

There was an awkward silence. They did not know this boy's name, or which god they should talk to on his behalf, and their sadness at his death was mixed with a guilty relief that it was not Li under the stones.

Finally, Paulo sat down beside the cairn and began to

speak, not to any god, but straight to the boy. He kept it simple, as though they were friends sitting side by side, passing the time on a lazy summer's day.

'It is a good place here, behind the rise. You have found the only shade on the whole plain. The sky is blue. The wind smells fresh and sweet after the storm. There is a sandstone bluff to the north and your village lies to the south, not too far away. Not too far at all. You will be fine, resting here in this good place for a while. When we have found your little brother, we will come back for you and take you home, I promise. We will bring you both home.'

Paulo rose to his feet again and looked around at the others. 'Will that do?' he asked, slightly unnerved by the silence.

Amber stepped forward, went up on her toes and kissed him on the cheek.

'It was OK,' said Hex, clearing his throat.

'Come on,' said Alex gruffly, keeping his head down. 'Let's move out. We have promises to keep.'

Alpha Force travelled on through the growing heat of the day, following the Unimog tracks. Sitting astride the quads with only their desert clothes to protect them against the soaring temperatures and drying wind, they were risking severe dehydration, but they had to catch up with Li. Now that she no longer had the tracker device, there was a real chance that she would disappear into slavery before they could find her. Once she was sold, Li would be very hard to trace and her future would not be pleasant. She could become a prisoner in a back-street hovel, weaving carpets in bad light until her eyes gave out and her lungs became clogged with the

104

fibre-filled air. She might end up as an unpaid servant in a private household or be forced to work in the sex industry. The thought of Li having to suffer any of these fates was enough to spur them on despite the rising temperature. The Scorpion's tracks headed north like an arrow, only swerving off course once to divert around the western side of the sandstone bluff that rose out of the plain like the back of a huge whale. Alpha Force stopped there for a water break and for Amber to waymark the bluff on her GPS unit.

'Why did they go that way?' asked Alex, frowning at the Unimog's tracks veering off to the west. 'It would've been quicker to cut round the eastern side of the bluff.'

'Yeah, but if they'd gone east, they would have been in full view of that,' said Amber, pointing out an oil installation that squatted out on the plain to the eastern side of the bluff. 'Security is tight around those places, and the last thing the Scorpion wanted was a bunch of armed guards coming out to investigate him.'

While the others drank their share of water from the girba, Alex took his binoculars from his pannier and focused on the drilling post. The gas burn-off reared above the pumps like a vast, smoky candle and black pipes stretched to the horizon, carrying away oil that had formed from sediments deposited at the bottom of a Saharan ocean four hundred million years earlier. A small cluster of Nissen-type huts and steel cargo boxes sat inside a fenced compound about the size of a football pitch, with a helicopter pad off to one side. Alex guessed that the oil men were housed in those huts, in air-conditioned comfort.

Amber was right, he noted. Both the compound and

the wells were patrolled by armed men. As Alex watched, he caught the flash of sun on binoculars. One of the guards was scanning the plain around the installation. Hurriedly, Alex lowered his own binoculars, suddenly feeling very exposed.

'Let's move on,' he said, anxious to get out of sight behind the bluff.

They kept close to the base of the bluff, glad of the shade it provided for them as they travelled through the hottest part of the day. The sandstone had been carved into fantastic shapes by the wind and the walls were dotted with caves. It took them half an hour to travel the length of the bluff, then they were out of its shade and back in the full heat of the desert sun, but they kept going, determined to catch up with Li before night fell.

The sun was low and the shadows long when Amber slapped Alex on the shoulder. Alex jumped. He had fallen into an almost trance-like condition as he followed the Unimog tracks through the desert with the sun beating down on his head.

'Border!' yelled Amber.

'What?'

'Border coming up! Stop!'

Alex brought the quad to a halt and Paulo pulled up beside him. Amber showed them the map on her GPS unit. The border was clearly marked on the little screen, but there was nothing ahead of them to show that they were about to cross over into Morocco; just the flat plain with the Unimog tracks cutting across it towards a range of low dunes. Alex lifted his binoculars and scanned the area.

'What are you expecting to see?' drawled Hex. 'A red

line marking the border? Or maybe a little checkpoint, just for us?'

'There might be soldiers,' said Alex.

'Out here?' Hex snorted. 'Why would they be out here? There isn't even a road. That's why the Scorpion came this way.'

'I know it's unlikely,' said Alex tightly. 'But it would be stupid to head into danger unprepared.'

'But that was just what you let Li do,' said Paulo. 'Wasn't it?'

The three of them glared at one another. They knew they should stop, but they were all feeling tired and dehydrated and wanting to take it out on someone.

'Guys, back down!' yelled Amber. 'Can we focus, please? According to my GPS unit, there's a town over the other side of those dunes. It's in Morocco, but only just.' She grinned at them. 'A frontier town. If I were the Scorpion that's the location I'd chose for my base. I think that town is where he's taken Li and the others. We're nearly there!'

Paulo smiled for the first time since Li had gone missing. 'Let us go,' he said.

The town was just where Amber had said it would be, spread out beyond the dunes like a 3D map. Alpha Force lay on their bellies at the top of a dune, studying the layout. The only road to the town came in from the north. To the south, there was nothing but desert, with the Unimog's tracks cutting across it. The town was built beside a large oasis. Unlike the dying well back at the village, this oasis was green and thriving. There was a large palmery around the edge, full of the feathery tops of date palms. Further in, there were terraces of olive, almond and fruit trees. Looking through his binoculars, Alex could even see grain and vegetable crops planted beneath the trees.

'There must be a big reserve of underground water here,' he muttered, studying the oasis.

'Forget the water,' said Amber, snatching the binoculars. 'Is there any sign of the Unimog?'

'You won't see it from up here, even with binoculars,' said Hex. 'There are too many alleyways and courtyards where it could be hidden.'

Amber threw him a look, then raked the binoculars back and forth across the town. Hex was right, of course. The houses were the white, flat-roofed buildings typical of the area and they all had deep courtyards to provide shade. Amber shifted the binoculars to the busy souk in the centre of the town. She could see hole-in-the-wall shops and market stalls and people thronging the streets, enjoying the relative cool of the early evening.

'That's where we should go,' she said, handing the binoculars back to Alex. 'The souk. The market. They sell everything there. If we want to know about slaves for sale, that's the place to find out.'

Sixteen

The Scorpion unlaced the canvas at the back of the Unimog and yanked open the flaps, making everyone blink in the sudden brightness.

'We have arrived,' he said.

It was four long hours since they had left Hakim bleeding and screaming in the desert. The shocked group in the back of the Unimog had needed no more convincing from Li of the Scorpion's intention to sell them into slavery. As the vehicle rattled on through the desert, they had clustered around Li and Khalid in the hot, stinking darkness, demanding to know the escape plan. Khalid had proudly told them all about Alpha Force, explaining that Li's friends Alex, Amber, Hex and Paulo were tracking the Unimog to the Scorpion's base, where they would carry out their rescue plan.

Li had smiled and nodded in agreement, but underneath her smiles she was much less confident of rescue. She had not told Khalid that she had left her tracker device out in the desert with Hakim. And there was another problem. The sandstorm. She knew it must have delayed Alpha Force, but by how much? Even if they managed to find her without the tracker device, would they get there before the auction?

'Out! Out now!' yelled the Scorpion, gesturing impatiently at them.

Li gave the others an encouraging smile before climbing stiffly down from the back of the Unimog. Quickly, she scanned the quiet back street, but there was no sign of the other four.

The Unimog was parked beside a high, whitewashed wall. There was an arched, wrought-iron gate in the wall and the Scorpion pushed it open, hustling them through into an enclosed courtyard with a well in the centre. Li looked around as the gate clanged shut behind them. This was the Scorpion's base. It was a long, low building, stretching around the other three sides of the courtyard. The side to the right of the gate was open to the courtyard and Li could see that it was one big, rectangular room with elaborate rugs scattered across the floor. On the rugs were low tables, set with hookahs, bowls of dates and pistachios and glasses with sprigs of mint in them, waiting for green tea. Cushions had been laid out around the tables to serve as seats. It could have been a room prepared for a party.

Except for the raised dais at one end.

Li stared at the platform and realized she was looking at the auction room where they were to be sold the next day. A shudder ran through her as she imagined standing on the dais while a roomful of buyers bid for her. Turning away, she scanned the left-hand wing of the building. This side was not open to the courtyard. The frontage was a windowless, whitewashed wall, with a stout, padlocked wooden door set into it. Li had a feeling that the room beyond that door was to be their quarters for the night.

The silence in the courtyard was broken by the sound of a high-pitched, complaining voice coming from the house that formed the main part of the building. The

110

voice came closer, accompanied by the slip-slap of leather sandals on tiles. They all looked towards the dark, open doorway of the house and a few seconds later the owner of the voice and the sandals appeared.

She was a huge woman, with a broad face as worn and pocked as a piece of old sandstone. She was dressed in black from head to foot, but her sleeves were rolled to the elbow, showing massive, slab-like forearms. As she came into the courtyard, a non-stop stream of Arabic flowed out of her, mainly directed at the Scorpion and his men. The Scorpion ignored her. He was tending to his dog in a shady corner.

'What's she saying?' whispered Li in French, turning to Khalid.

'She is his mother. She is saying that he is late. She has only two hours to make us ready before the buyers arrive.'

'The buyers! But the auction isn't until tomorrow.'

'No. But tonight there is a viewing. They are coming to look at us before they buy.'

The woman marched up to them, still complaining, and roughly pushed them into a line. She inspected them, tutting when she came to Khalid. She grabbed hold of his chin and turned his head from side to side, inspecting the scarring before she moved on down the line.

'What did she say?' whispered Li, once she had been inspected.

'She says I will fetch less. But I don't need a pretty face to weave carpets,' said Khalid matter-of-factly.

Li felt the anger race through her at this casual cruelty. She narrowed her eyes and glared at the woman as she waddled on down the line. 'She's no oil painting,' she hissed and Khalid grinned.

111

'How can you smile at a time like this?' demanded Li, staring at Khalid's cheerful face.

'Because we will escape tonight,' said Khalid calmly. 'Alpha Force will make sure of that.'

As Li stared at Khalid, she wished she could be so sure. At the other end of the line the woman's complaints had turned into shouts and they both turned to see what was happening. She had hauled a bucketful of water from the well and plonked it down in front of Juma, who was at the head of the line. As Li and Khalid watched, the woman handed Juma a metal dipper.

'*Yallah!*' she shouted. '*Yallah! Yallah!*'

When Juma did not move fast enough for her, she pulled a thin, whippy cane from her belt and began beating him across the back of the legs with it. Juma yelled with pain and surprise. Quickly, Khalid translated for him. 'She's saying "Come on, let's go!" She wants you to pick up the water.'

Juma grabbed the bucket handle and the woman stopped beating him. 'Now take it down the line and give everyone a drink,' translated Khalid.

The water was cool and clear. After two days in the desert, drinking from goatskin girbas, Li thought it was the best water she had ever tasted. While they drank, the woman moved to the side of the courtyard, still complaining. She took the covers from two large bowls and beckoned them over. Everyone jumped to obey her, but she still used her cane to hurry them along.

'She says we must eat quickly,' explained Khalid.

The larger bowl was full of cold, stuck-together couscous and the smaller bowl contained some sort of a watery stew with swirls of grease floating on the top. Li peered more closely at the stew and wished she hadn't.

She could see pieces of liver in there, and part of a heart, with the white tube of artery still sticking out of it. She felt her stomach turn over at the thought of eating cold offal stew, but the others were already tucking in, sitting around the bowls in a tight circle and eating with their hands. Only Samir was not eating. He sat, staring straight ahead, his eyes big and strained in his thin face and his mind full of images of his brother's fate. Sisi leaned across and pushed morsels of food into his mouth, feeding him as though he were a baby bird. Li forced herself to sit down with them and eat a few handfuls of the couscous.

'Here,' said Kesia, holding out a dripping piece of lung.

'No,' said Li, feeling her stomach clench. 'Thanks.'

Kesia shrugged and ate the morsel herself. Li felt ashamed at her distaste. Her companions were very hungry. They had been existing on flat bread and water for days. Besides, it was only Li's western upbringing that was making her feel sick; the others saw nothing wrong in using every part of an animal. In their communities, when a beast was slaughtered, not a single scrap was wasted.

While they were eating, the Scorpion and his men disappeared into the house, leaving the woman in charge. By the time the bowls were empty she had drawn another bucket of water and was standing beside it, holding a large scrubbing brush and a bar of hard soap. She shouted across the courtyard at them.

'She says girls first,' translated Khalid.

The boys sat against the wall on the left-hand side of the courtyard while the girls lined up in front of the woman. Kesia was at the head of the line. The woman

113

grabbed her and began to strip off her clothes. Kesia resisted, casting horrified glances towards the line of watching boys, but the woman beat her with the cane until she stopped struggling. Kesia hung her head and tears of shame dripped from the end of her nose as she allowed the woman to strip her. An uncomfortable silence grew in the courtyard, broken only by the sound of Kesia's sobs.

Li was horrified. The woman was stripping Kesia of more than her clothes; her human dignity was being stripped away too. Li looked over to the line of boys. They were all embarrassed, staring at the ground or studying their hands. Suddenly, Khalid's face brightened as an idea came to him. He glanced at the other boys, then shuffled around until he was sitting with his back to Kesia. Hastily, the other boys copied Khalid. They all turned to face the wall and stayed there, staring at the whitewashed surface as though it were the most fascinating thing they had ever seen.

When Kesia saw what the boys were doing, her sobs stopped and a relieved smile spread across her face. She straightened her shoulders and stood proudly, meeting the woman's gaze. The woman tutted, grabbed Kesia by the neck and dunked her head into the bucket. Kesia came up coughing and spluttering and the woman attacked her hair with the hard soap. Next she lathered the brush and scrubbed Kesia all over with it, ignoring her winces of pain. Finally, the bucket of water was upended over Kesia's head and the woman handed her a simple, round-necked cotton tunic with holes for her arms. Kesia pulled on the tunic, which came down to her knees, and went to sit in the sun to dry off.

Jumoke was next. She cried as the harsh bristles

114

scraped her skin, but the woman beat her with the cane until she stopped. When Li stepped up for her turn, she understood why Jumoke had cried. It felt as though the bristles were tearing her to shreds and the soap was harsh and stinging. Once it was over, Li tried to pick up her gandourah and sirwal, but the woman slapped her hard and thrust a tunic at her instead. Li glared at the woman, the anger flaring inside her again, but the woman stared back at her with eyes as hard and cold as a pair of black marbles until Li lowered her gaze.

I will pay you back for this, thought Li as she pulled on the tunic and went to join the other girls. Just you wait.

Seventeen

'They're all staring at you!' hissed Amber to Hex and Alex, as Alpha Force walked towards the souk.

They had left their quads in a quiet side street on the outskirts of the town. In their travel-stained headcloths, gandourah and sirwal, they had hoped to merge in with the crowd, but things were not quite working out. Amber could easily be one of the many West Africans living and working in Morocco, and Paulo's dark, South American looks meant he could just about pass as an Arab if nobody looked too closely, but Hex and Alex were causing problems. Their fair skin labelled them as westerners, but their desert clothes gave out a different message and the street traders and gangs of little boys trying to sell baskets of dates did not quite know how to react to them.

'What do you suggest, Amber?' replied Alex, trying to keep his head down and his grey eyes hidden as he walked.

'I don't know, but we'll never find out where they've taken Li while you're getting this sort of attention!'

'Wait here,' said Hex suddenly, grabbing Alex by the arm and pulling him down a narrow alleyway.

Amber and Paulo moved to the side of the street and leaned against the wall as though they had nothing better to do than watch the crowds pass by. The date

116

boys lost interest and moved on, the street traders turned to more promising customers and still Hex and Alex did not reappear.

After a few more minutes Amber turned to peer into the alleyway. Two women dressed in all-enveloping black burkas were approaching her, but otherwise the alleyway was empty. 'Where are they?' she sighed.

'Right here,' said one of the women in a deep voice, gripping Amber by the elbow.

Amber squeaked and peered in through the cloth grille in the front of the burka. Hex's amused green eyes looked out at her.

'Where did you find those?' gasped Amber.

'Washing lines are useful things,' said Hex, still gripping Amber by the arm as they walked into the souk. 'You'll have to guide me though. I can't see left or right in this thing. Can't even see my own feet. I feel as though I'm going to fall over something any minute now.'

Behind Amber and Hex, Paulo took Alex by the arm and the four of them made their way into the centre of the souk. No-one paid any attention to the two women in burkas being accompanied through the streets by their young sons. Amber led them from stall to stall, pretending to inspect the displays of semi-precious stones, jewellery, pottery, carpets, leather, brasswork and spices. All the while, she was listening to the buzz of voices and homing in on any conversations in French.

They were passing a small street café when Amber came to a sudden halt. Alex walked straight into the back of her. 'Give me a bit of warning, will you?' he whispered from under his burka.

'Shhh!' hissed Amber, tilting her head. Someone was

talking about an auction. She looked in the direction of the voices and saw two Arab men sitting at a small table in the corner, drinking glasses of tea. A slow grin spread across Amber's face as she listened.

'We've found her!' she whispered to the others. 'Those two are talking about a beautiful Chinese girl who will be sold at auction tomorrow. That must be Li. There's a viewing tonight and they're going to have a look at her once they've finished their tea. All we need to do is follow them!'

The men led them back out to the southern outskirts of the town. As they walked, more men joined the two they were following and by the time they arrived in a quiet back street right on the edge of the desert, there was a small crowd of potential buyers. The men all strolled through an arched gateway set into a high, white-washed wall. Amber nudged Hex in the ribs and nodded towards the dusty Unimog, parked out on the street beside the wall. The Scorpion's men were working on it, swilling out the back and loading new supplies into the spaces under the benches.

'This is it,' she whispered. 'And it looks like they're planning another buying trip after the auction. Huh! That's what they think. Come on.' She marched up to the gate with Hex clutching her arm and Paulo and Alex hurrying along behind, but the Scorpion stepped in front of her, barring her way.

'Buyers only,' he snapped, folding his arms. He was wearing a fresh pair of jeans and a different checked shirt. His cowboy boots were polished to a high shine and his scorpion tattoo glistened on his forearm, the stinger seeming to move whenever the muscles flexed.

His curved knife hung at his belt in its leather sheath. Amber stepped back meekly, guiding Hex away from the gate, and the Scorpion dismissed her. Turning to his men, he gave a sharp whistle and pointed to his watch. They were ready to start the viewing.

The two men hurried into the courtyard and the Scorpion shut the gate. Alpha Force moved cautiously back up to the closed gate, expecting to be shooed away, but nobody paid them any attention. It seemed that curious onlookers were a common sight at the gate on viewing evenings.

The buyers settled on their cushions in the open-sided auction room and the Scorpion moved around, shaking hands and greeting old clients. A huge woman dressed in black was easing her bulk between the low tables and bending to pour green tea into the men's glasses. Alex shook his head as he watched the scene in the courtyard. It all looked so civilized, but these men were there to trade in human beings.

The woman finished pouring tea and, at a signal from the Scorpion, waddled over to a stout wooden door on the opposite side of the courtyard. The hum of conversation died and the men all turned to watch as the woman unlocked the padlock and swung the door open. She pulled a cruel-looking switch from her belt and shouted through the doorway in a high-pitched voice.

'Yallah! Yallah!'

The men all craned their necks and then relaxed back on to their cushions as six boys walked from the dark room beyond the doorway and stood blinking in the courtyard. The Scorpion knew who the men had come to see and he was saving the main attraction for last. There was a lot of good-natured laughter from the

119

buyers. The tea was hot. The dates were sweet. They were happy to play along.

'This is disgusting,' muttered Amber, glaring at the buyers.

'You're looking the wrong way,' whispered Hex. Amber followed his pointing finger and saw that one of the six boys in the courtyard was Khalid. She grinned and tried to catch his eye, but Khalid was too busy sending wary glances over at the buyers. The woman brought her switch down over his shoulders and he jumped, then hurried across the courtyard, keeping a firm grip on the hand of a young Arab boy.

'That's the kid from the village,' said Alex and Amber nodded, recognizing him. Paulo watched him intently, remembering the promise he had made to the boy's older brother to bring him home again.

One by one, the boys were hustled up on to the platform at the front of the auction room. They were all wearing identical pairs of coarse cotton trousers and their chests were bare. The buyers studied them and occasionally called out a request to the woman in black. She would nod and get the boy to turn round, or run on the spot or hold his hands out with the fingers spread. Once she switched on a torch and shone it into a boy's open mouth so that the buyers could see his teeth.

When all the boys had been viewed, they were lined up to one side of the stage and three West African girls, two older and one younger, were brought out of the dark room across the courtyard. They were dressed in short, sleeveless tunics and their feet were bare. The girls went through the same viewing procedure as the boys, then they too were lined up at the side of the stage.

A rustle of whispering spread through the buyers. The girl they had come to see was to be brought out next.

Amber, Alex, Paulo and Hex turned to watch the dark doorway. The woman called, then called again, but it wasn't until she brought out her switch and flourished it threateningly that the final girl stepped out of the room. It was Li. She was dressed like the other girls in a sleeveless shift, but she wore it as though it were a royal gown.

Paulo felt his heart swell with pride as he watched her stalk across the courtyard with her head held high and her uptilted eyes flashing defiance. She looked beautiful. Her long hair swung loose, reaching down to her waist. It was still slightly damp and it shone with glossy highlights as it caught the evening sun. Her skin looked a little red, as though it had been scrubbed too hard, but otherwise Paulo was glad to see that she looked unharmed. Behind Paulo, Alex let out a long, relieved sigh. He had never quite forgiven himself for letting her go off with the Scorpion in the first place.

Li stepped up on to the dais and stood with her hands on her hips, glaring out at the men who sat at the low tables. The murmur of voices rose in volume to an excited buzz, and suddenly hands were being waved in the air as the buyers called out their offers. The Scorpion smiled, then walked up to the front of the room and stood there, shaking his head and holding up his hands. He gave a nod to the woman and she began herding the group back across the courtyard.

'Come on, Li,' breathed Paulo. 'Look this way. This way.'

As though she had heard him, Li turned her head to look out at the street. Her eyes widened in delighted astonishment as she saw Amber and Paulo standing at the gate, grinning in at her. Li turned her attention to the two burka-clad women standing behind Amber and Paulo and her look of delight turned into a puzzled frown until one of the women gave her a thumbs-up sign. Li smiled in sudden understanding, then gave a slight nod towards the dark room before facing forwards again and walking on across the courtyard.

'There must be a window round the side,' muttered Hex. 'She wouldn't've nodded like that otherwise.'

'Then let us find it,' said Paulo.

They followed the street as it curved round to the right and there it was, a glassless, barred window in the back wall of the Scorpion's slave quarters. The window was at street level, so they squatted down in the dust with their backs to the wall as though they were just taking a short rest.

'You took your time,' said Li from the other side of the window.

'Please, you do not need to thank us, Li,' grinned Paulo. 'We know you are grateful.'

He peered in through the window. The room on the other side of the bars was below street level, so the window was above head height for Li and she was having to look up in order to see him. Khalid was standing next to her, smiling broadly. The other children were gathered around Li and Khalid, their eyes full of a wary hope.

Li smiled at Paulo, then her face became serious again. 'Hakim?' she asked. 'Did you find him?'

'Yes,' said Paulo.

'And?'

'I am sorry, Li. He was dead.'

122

Li bowed her head. Behind her, Samir gave a wordless cry and sat down suddenly on one of the filthy foam mattresses that were spread on the floor. He did not understand English, but he had picked out his brother's name and he could hear the tone of their voices and see the looks on their faces.

'We have to get this guy!' hissed Li, raising her head again. Her eyes were full of tears.

'No problem,' said Alex. 'Now we know where his base is, we'll go to the police and—'

'Useless,' interrupted Li. 'He had a group of the local worthies round to tea this afternoon, including the boss policeman. He's bribing them all to turn a blind eye. We're on our own.'

'OK,' said Alex, trying not to let his dismay show on his face. 'OK.'

'You will be able to get us out of here?' asked Li.

'Of course we will,' said Amber, raising her eyebrows at Hex. 'Tell her the plan, Hex.'

'The plan. Right.' Hex frowned, thinking hard. He reached out and picked at the wall where the window bars were set. Under the whitewash, the wall was of a mud-brick construction and it broke into dry flakes where his fingernail scraped at it. His face cleared and he turned to Paulo. 'That Unimog round the corner – could you hot-wire it?'

'No problem,' said Paulo promptly.

'OK,' said Hex. 'This is how it's going to be.'

Eighteen

The full moon shone down through the window bars, casting pale squares of light over Samir and Jumoke as they slept huddled together on one of the foam mattresses. They were the only two properly asleep. The others all sat around the edges of the room with their backs against the wall, alternately dozing then starting awake and staring up at the barred window.

Li was as jumpy as a cat. Paulo and the others had promised her they would be back once everything was quiet. The Scorpion and his guests had stayed up late, enjoying the cool of the night in the courtyard, but the last buyer had left two hours ago and, from what she could see through a crack in the wooden door of their prison, Li judged that the house had been dark and quiet for over an hour. Where were they?

She sighed and tilted her head back, banging it gently against the rough wall as though she could knock away the thoughts she was having. She was imagining all sorts of different scenarios which all ended in the same way. Alpha Force did not return to rescue them and the auction went ahead the next morning; Alex would decide that the town police could not all be corrupt and persuade the other three to go to the police station with him . . .

Li gave her head an extra-hard bang against the wall

to stop that thought. 'Come on!' she hissed, staring up at the window. She hated being a prisoner. The room was dark and bare, apart from a selection of filthy foam mattresses and a large bucket in one corner, which served as a toilet. Most of the children had had to use the bucket after their meal of cold offal, and the smell in the room was getting pretty bad. But even if her prison had been as luxurious as a five-star hotel room, Li would still have hated it. The bars were what she hated, and the locked door that she could not open.

One piece of luck had come their way. The Scorpion's mother had been so rushed getting them ready for the viewing, she was still clearing up the courtyard as the first buyers were arriving. She had hustled Li and the others into the room and had hastily gathered up all their clothes, sandals and boots, throwing the bundles in after them. After the viewing she had locked them back in the room, forgetting all about the clothes she had thrown in earlier.

Li had not relished the idea of attempting to escape in bare feet and wearing nothing but a tunic. She had climbed back into her own clothes gratefully, feeling as though she were claiming back a part of herself. With her hair tucked up into her headcloth and her sturdy desert boots on her feet, she felt ready for anything. Except this endless waiting.

Suddenly a shadow moved in front of the window, blocking out the moonlight. Li sprang to her feet and hurried over. Alex was there and he was carrying a length of chain. The links clinked together quietly as he threaded them carefully back and forth through the window bars.

'There's a dog in the courtyard,' he whispered to Li.

'We reckon that as soon as Paulo hot-wires the Unimog, the dog will start to bark, so we'll have to move fast after that.'

Li nodded. 'I'll get them ready.'

Quickly, she woke Jumoke and Samir and took them over to join the others at the back of the room. While each of them grabbed one of the stinking foam mattresses and held it in front of them like a shield, Li hurried back to the window.

Outside, Alex had finished threading the chain through the bars. He picked up the two end links and backed into the street, dragging the double length of chain with him. Once the chain was laid out ready, Alex hurried to the corner to give Paulo the thumbs-up signal.

Amber and Hex appeared at the window. 'All right,' whispered Amber. 'We're gonna get out of the way until Paulo's done his stuff, but then we'll be straight back to help you guys out of there. OK?'

'OK,' grinned Li.

Amber reached through the bars and squeezed Li's hand, then she and Hex moved off, slipping through the shadowy street like a pair of ghosts. Li hurried over to the far wall and grabbed her mattress shield.

A few seconds later the Unimog's engine started up. Instantly, the Scorpion's dog started barking in the courtyard. The barks became louder as the big vehicle moved away from the courtyard gate. Li heard the engine note grow louder as Paulo turned the big vehicle into the street outside the window. She heard the clink of the chain as Alex slipped the two ends over the tow hook on the back of the Unimog, then the clunk of the cab door as he climbed into the vehicle to join Paulo.

'Here we go,' she whispered.

Paulo put the Unimog into gear, revved the big engine and started forward. The twin lengths of chain slithered through the dust like snakes, then lifted into the air and straightened, vibrating with tension. Paulo leaned from the cab window, watching the wall of Li's prison. Nothing was moving, so he pressed down on the accelerator, pulling more power from the engine. The window bars groaned and cracks began to spider through the wall where the bars were set, but still the window held.

The Scorpion's dog was barking frantically now and the door next to Li shuddered as the beast threw itself against the wood. Li jumped, then peeped out from behind her mattress shield, willing Paulo to hurry up. The bricks around the window were grating together and avalanches of dust were falling from the holes around the window bars. Surely it must give soon?

Outside, Paulo was pushing the engine hard and blue smoke was pouring from the exhaust into the moonlit street.

'*Dios*,' he muttered. 'It must happen now. The towing hook will not hold much longer.'

He made an all-or-nothing decision and floored the accelerator. The Unimog roared, the wheels spun, and suddenly a whole section of brickwork, with the window bars at the centre, exploded out of the prison wall. The Unimog leaped forward with the chunk of wall dragging behind it and Paulo had to do a fast bit of steering to avoid crashing into the side of the house opposite.

In the prison room, Li ducked back behind the mattress as lumps of brickwork flew through the air like shrapnel. In the courtyard the dog flung itself against the door again and again. Its barks had turned into one long, baying howl and, as Li scrambled to her feet, she heard men's voices above the howl.

'Quick!' she yelled, heading for the hole in the wall where the window had been. She took up position at one side of the hole and Khalid ran to the other side. Amber and Hex appeared, taking up similar positions in the street. As Alex scrambled from the cab to unhook the chain from the Unimog, Li and Khalid grabbed Jumoke and boosted her up to Amber and Hex.

Alex jumped on to the footplate of the cab and hung there as Paulo backed the Unimog up to the wall again.

'That's it!' yelled Alex. 'You're there!'

Paulo braked but kept the engine running. Alex climbed into the cab and Jumoke clambered into the back of the waiting vehicle as Li and Khalid boosted Samir through the hole in the wall after her. Kesia and Sisi followed in quick succession.

Light flooded the courtyard and sent thin streamers through the wooden door of their prison. Li heard the thud of running feet as the Scorpion and his men headed across the courtyard. Her heart sank as she and Khalid grabbed Zaid and lifted him up to Amber and Hex.

'They're on their way!' she yelled, grabbing Rafiki by the arms. 'We're not all going to get out in time.'

'Don't worry about that,' grunted Hex as he yanked Rafiki through the hole. 'They're going to have a bit of trouble opening the gate.'

Li heard the wrought-iron gate in the courtyard wall clang, then clang again as the Scorpion yanked at the latch. She grinned as she hauled Ajani up into Hex's waiting hands. 'What did you do?'

'Padlock and chain,' said Hex. 'They'll need bolt cutters to open it.'

As Li turned to get Juma, the high-pitched voice of the Scorpion's mother was added to the yells of the men in the courtyard. Her bulk blocked out the streamers of light and the door shook as she grabbed hold of the padlock on the other side. A key chain rattled.

'Let's go!' yelled Li.

Juma shook his head. 'You first,' he said.

'Juma! Now!' yelled Li.

Juma shook his head again. 'You next,' he said stubbornly.

Li did not have time to argue. As the key slotted into the padlock on the other side of the door, she got Juma in a headlock and pinned his arms behind his back. 'Lift!' she yelled to Khalid and together they boosted a surprised Juma up to Amber and Hex.

'Now you,' panted Li, bending down and forming her clasped hands into a foothold. Khalid did not argue. He stepped up on to her hands and she boosted him out into the street.

As Li stepped back, preparing to jump up, grab hold of the edge of the hole and pull herself up by her strong fingers, the door swung open behind her and the Scorpion's mother burst into the room. With a shriek, the woman ran towards Li as she jumped. Li's fingers gripped the edge of the hole and Amber and Hex reached down to grab her wrists, but the woman caught her by the ankles and yanked her back down into the room.

Li fell hard. The wind was knocked out of her and she sprawled on the floor, trying to pull some air into her lungs. She felt a sharp pain sear across her cheek as the woman began to beat her around the head with her cane. As the cane came down again and again, Li felt a red-hot fury boiling up inside her. She filled her lungs and surged to her feet with a yell. The top of her head connected with the woman's chin. There was a loud clack as the woman's jaw snapped shut. She staggered back a few steps but did not fall.

Calmly, Li went into a fighting stance. She chose her moves, then launched herself into the air. Her booted foot slammed into the woman's stomach, making her fold forward. Li landed lightly and brought her hand slicing down into the side of the woman's neck. Instantly, the woman dropped to the floor, her huge bulk hitting the hard-packed ground with a solid thud.

'Come on, Li!' yelled Hex from the street, but Li hadn't finished yet. She picked up the toilet bucket and dumped the stinking contents over the woman's head.

'Try getting that off with a scrubbing brush,' snarled Li.

She ran for the wall and jumped, soaring high into the air. Her feet connected with the brickwork and she powered her way up the vertical surface, seeming to defy gravity. Her strong fingers got a hold on the crumbling bottom edge of the hole and she hauled herself up. She rolled out into the dark street and came up on the balls of her feet. As she ran for the Unimog, she heard the thud of running feet coming towards the corner. The Scorpion and his men must have clambered over the gate. She found some extra strength, sprinted for the back of the Unimog and threw herself in. Paulo slammed his foot down on the accelerator and the vehicle screeched off down the street, sending sprays of dust and dirt from its spinning tyres.

Li grabbed on to the end of the bench seat and hauled herself up to look out through the canvas flaps. The Scorpion and his men had rounded the corner and the men were lifting their Kalashnikovs to their shoulders.

'Get down!' yelled Li.

They all fell to the floor of the truck as the bullets began to fly, whining through the canvas and clanging into the metal base. Li screamed. If this stream of bullets kept up, someone was going to die.

Then she heard the Scorpion shout an order and the bullets stopped. Cautiously she raised her head as the Unimog rattled on down the street; a snarling mouthful of fangs rose up over the tailgate, snatching at her face. Li yanked her head back as the Scorpion's dog scrabbled against the truck before falling back to the road. That was why the Scorpion had ordered his men to stop firing. He did not want his dog to be hit.

The dog kept chasing, but it was falling behind. Li began to think they were going to get away, but just before the Unimog careered around the corner she saw the Scorpion and his men running towards a battered jeep.

Nineteen

Paulo's face was a mask of concentration as he steered the big vehicle through the narrow, twisting streets. He had checked out the route earlier that evening, but it was dark now and everything looked different. He thought he was heading towards the edge of town, but as the minutes ticked by and the desert did not appear he began to wonder whether he could be steering them further and further into the centre. He sighed with relief as he turned a final corner and the Unimog shot out into the open spaces of the desert.

He reached for the night-vision goggles he had retrieved from his quad pannier and slammed them down over his eyes. Instantly, the bumps and troughs that had been hidden by shadow and moonlight sprang into view. Paulo settled back in his seat and turned the Unimog south, setting a course that would take them past the edge of the dunes.

A sudden noise made him jump. Someone was banging on the back of the cab. He began to slow down, but the banging became more frantic, as though it were trying to tell him to keep going. Paulo peered out at his wing mirror and his eyes widened. 'Uh-oh,' he said. 'We have a problem.'

Alex looked in his mirror and saw a jeep careering across the desert towards them. The Scorpion was driving and his two men were standing up in the back, hanging on to the roll bars. As Alex watched, they lifted their Kalashnikovs and rested them on the top of the bars.

'They're going to start firing!' he yelled.

'Hang on, everyone,' shouted Paulo.

As the bullets started to whine around the Unimog, Paulo turned the wheel back and forth, making the big vehicle swerve crazily from side to side. This made them less of an easy target for the men in the back of the jeep, who were themselves struggling to hang on at the same time as firing their weapons. The problem was that the jeep was gaining ground all the time. The jeep was a faster vehicle than the lumbering Unimog and the Scorpion was driving a straight course. With every swerve that Paulo took, the jeep gained a few metres on them.

'It's not working!' yelled Alex. 'They're going to catch up with us!'

Paulo nodded grimly. He looked over at the dunes to his left, then suddenly turned the big truck towards them and put his foot down.

Alex ducked as a bullet shattered his window and embedded itself in the dashboard. As he sat up again, shaking his head to get the glass splinters out of his hair, another bullet clipped his wing mirror and ricocheted off into the night. Alex flattened himself against his seat back. His heart was beating so quickly, it felt as though it was about to jump out of his chest. He had never felt so exposed. As the dune loomed closer, filling the windscreen, he tried not to think about what a bullet would do to him.

In the back of the Unimog, they were even more

exposed. Everyone was flattened on the floor of the truck, clinging on to the bench supports and each other as the bullets whined overhead, ripping through the canvas cover. Jumoke was clinging to Khalid's neck and he curled himself around her, trying to shield her from the bullets. Hex was lying across Amber and Li was doing her best to shelter Samir. The truck bed was jarring and shuddering, bouncing them up and down on the wooden slats of the floor until they felt scraped and bruised all over.

When the Unimog hit the dune slope, the truck bed tilted upwards violently and suddenly they were all sliding towards the tailgate, scrabbling for a hand-hold. Li wedged her foot under the bench support and braced herself as Kesia came sliding down on top of her. Kesia began to pull herself off Li, but then she gave a sudden jerk and went limp. Li felt Kesia's weight slump against her and felt the slick warmth of blood seeping on to the back of her neck.

Kesia's blood.

Kesia had been hit.

Meanwhile Paulo had changed down and was pointing the nose of the Unimog straight up the steep face of the dune.

'What are you doing?' yelled Alex.

'Ground clearance,' shouted Paulo, urging the vehicle on towards the top of the slope. 'It is our only chance!'

The Unimog toiled up towards the crest of the dune in high second and the jeep followed behind, still gaining. Paulo stared at the top of the slope as his windscreen filled with sky, judging his moment. He was waiting for the instant when the front wheels of the big truck crested the dune. His face was set in a grimace as he concentrated on the feel of the pedals under his boots and listened for a change in the sound of the straining engine. They only had one chance and he must not misjudge it. If he eased off the accelerator too soon, they would slide helplessly back down the slope towards the Scorpion. If he overshot, the big vehicle would overbalance and roll over and over down the other side of the dune, crushing everyone in the back of the truck.

'Now,' he muttered to himself as the front wheels began to tip over the crest. He eased off the accelerator and the Unimog hung in the balance long enough to make the sweat pop out on his forehead. Then, slowly, the nose tilted to point down the far slope of the dune. Paulo sighed with relief and eased the Unimog forward. The first part of his plan had worked, but that would count for nothing if the second part failed.

'Watch the jeep!' he yelled to Alex as he concentrated on getting them down the dune slope in one piece.

Alex stuck his head out through his shattered window. Behind them, the jeep was just coming over the top of the dune. The front wheels rose up above the crest, then tilted downwards – and stopped. The men in the back of the jeep were thrown forward by the sudden stop, then back again as the jeep rocked the other way. One man went head over heels, disappearing down the slope the jeep had just climbed. The other overbalanced, knocking his head on the side of the vehicle and falling in a boneless heap in the sand. The jeep remained balanced on the crest of the dune, resting on its chassis with both its front and back wheels spinning uselessly in mid-air. The engine whined as the Scorpion tried to urge the jeep forward, but there was nothing for the tyres to grip and all that happened was that the chassis sank further into the soft sand.

'They've bellied-out,' reported Alex.

'Yes!' whooped Paulo, slamming his fist on to the steering wheel. The second part of his plan had worked. 'What did I tell you about this beauty? Ground clearance!'

His teeth shone white below the green lenses of his night-vision goggles as he gave Alex a brief grin and then turned back to the task of getting them safely down the dune. They reached the desert floor again and Paulo sent the Unimog roaring forward across the open ground. Alex looked behind him one more time and saw the Scorpion standing still and silent beside his bellied-out jeep, watching them go. Alex had a feeling they had not seen the last of him.

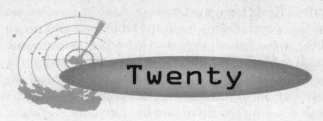

Twenty

Li looked deep into Kesia's eyes and spoke to her gently in French. 'Kesia. You have to be brave now, all right?'

'I will be as quick as I can,' said Paulo. 'It will not take long.'

Kesia closed her eyes and Sisi squeezed her hand while Li took a grip on her other arm and held it down for Paulo. The bullet had only clipped the arm, carving a channel through Kesia's bicep without hitting the bone. The entrance wound at the front of the arm was small and relatively neat, but the bullet had made a much bigger mess on the way out. It had blasted a splatter of flesh out ahead of it, tearing a large, ragged hole in the back of Kesia's arm as it exited.

Paulo had not dared to stop the Unimog until they were well away from the Scorpion. He had crossed the border into Algeria and driven grimly on through the night, with Kesia moaning and crying in the back of the vehicle. Amber and Li had bound her arm with strips of Amber's headcloth, but the wound would not stop bleeding and soon the makeshift bandage was soaked through.

Finally Paulo looked over to the eastern horizon and spotted the black outline of the sandstone bluff they had passed on the way in. He nodded in satisfaction and brought the Unimog to a halt behind a low rise. Hex, Amber and Khalid climbed the rise to keep watch for vehicles following from the north, while Li and Paulo gently lifted Kesia from the Unimog. Alex had pulled up a few of the wooden slats from the truck bed and made a small fire at the base of the rise. He had boiled up some water and added potassium permanganate from the medical kit in his survival tin. Finally, he had used his knife to cut strips from the remains of Amber's headcloth and dunked them into the pink, boiling water to sterilize them.

Now Paulo was about to clean the wound and attempt to stem the bleeding. He and Li had left Juma in charge of the fire, where he was now giving out many more orders than were necessary to brew up some tea. They had carried Kesia around to the front of the Unimog, bringing Sisi along to give her friend moral support. Paulo discreetly slipped Alex's knife blade into the potassium permanganate mixture to sterilize it in case it was needed, then he signalled to Alex up in the cab of the Unimog. Alex turned on the vehicle's headlights and the little group was suddenly bathed in bright, white light.

Kesia whimpered as Paulo leaned forward to inspect the wound in the glare of the headlights. It was still bleeding freely. Li was going to have to pinch the ragged edges of the wound together while he applied butterfly sutures from Alex's survival tin. Then he would bind the arm with the sterilized strips of cloth. But first, he had to clean the wound and, as he feared, he was going to need the knife. Fragments of cloth from Kesia's sleeve had been rammed into her flesh by the bullet and were now embedded in the wound. If he did not get them out, the dust-laden scraps of cloth would cause infection.

Paulo pulled the knife from the water and waited for

the blade to cool, then he nodded to Li, who gripped Kesia's arm more tightly. Paulo dug the point of the knife into the wound and hooked out a fragment of cloth. Kesia stiffened and screamed, then her eyes rolled up in her head and she passed out. Paulo was relieved. Back home on his ranch, he had cleaned up dreadful wounds on cattle that had caught themselves on barbed wire, but he had never had to do this to a young girl before. He set to work, quickly digging out all the embedded cloth while Kesia was still unconscious.

'There,' he said after a few minutes. 'Now we can clean it.' The potassium permanganate mixture was cool enough now for Paulo to lift out a strip of cloth with his fingers. He cleaned all around the wound, irrigating it well with the sterilized water.

'Now, Li, I want you to hold the edges together while I apply the sutures,' he said.

Li screwed up her face at the thought of touching the wound, but she did as she was told and Paulo quickly and expertly applied the sutures that would hold the wound together. Finally he bound up the arm with more strips of sterilized cloth.

'There. That is the best I can do. Now, we wait for her to wake up again, give her some tea and painkillers and head on towards Samir's village.'

Five minutes later Kesia was sitting up by the fire, sipping from a mug of sweet tea that Sisi was holding for her. She looked drawn and she was obviously in some pain but otherwise she was recovering well from her ordeal and the wound was now hardly bleeding at all.

'Your survival kit saves the day yet again,' teased Li, grinning at Alex.

139

'Will she be well enough to travel?' asked Alex, handing Kesia two painkilling tablets from his survival kit. 'She can sit up front in the cab.'

Li translated Alex's question and Kesia nodded and smiled. She would be well enough.

Juma and his gang of three took over the watch while Amber, Khalid and Hex came down for some tea, then Alex put out the fire and they all clambered wearily back into the Unimog. Amber had retrieved her GPS unit from her quad bike earlier that evening and packed it into a rucksack she had bought in the souk. She went in the front to keep Paulo headed on the right track. Kesia and Sisi sat between them in the high cab.

'Let us go,' said Paulo, flourishing the ignition key.

'Hey!' said Amber. 'Where'd you find that?'

'Behind the sun-visor,' grinned Paulo.

'So you didn't have to hot-wire it after all, back in the town?'

Paulo looked embarrassed. 'I did not find the key until we stopped here.'

Amber laughed. 'Don't you know to look there first? That's where they always find it in the movies.'

Paulo shrugged and turned the key. The engine coughed, then spluttered to a stop. Paulo frowned and tried again. Again the engine croaked a few times and died.

'What's wrong?' asked Amber.

Paulo tried a third time. A harsh grating noise came from the engine and dark smoke began to escape around the edges of the bonnet. 'I am not sure,' said Paulo. 'I think maybe the bullets caused some damage. Hold on, I will check.'

He reached down under the steering wheel and

pulled the bonnet release lever. The bonnet sprang open and a sudden explosion of flames shot out from beneath it, rising high into the air and licking against the windscreen.

Amber screamed as a gout of flame roared around the side of the windscreen and flared into the cab through her shattered side window. She flung herself back against the seat and felt the heat of the flame sear past her face, sizzling the hair above her forehead. Amber was terrified of fire. Her parents had both died in a burning plane. She turned to the door and kicked it open with the strength of panic, then she grabbed Sisi's arm with one hand and her rucksack with the other. Pulling Sisi after her, Amber jumped from the cab. They soared through the flames and landed some distance from the cab, rolling over and over on the stony ground.

Amber sat up and looked down at herself, then over to Sisi. She could not quite believe they had escaped unscathed. She looked back to the Unimog cab. It was full of flames.

'Paulo!' she screamed, scrambling to her feet and heading towards the burning cab.

'Here,' called Paulo, staggering towards her, carrying Kesia in his arms.

Amber gave a sob of relief, then rushed on past him, heading for the back of the Unimog. The flames were licking at the fuel tank behind the cab and she had to get the others out of the back. Alex was already opening the flaps and peering out, wondering what the problem was.

'Come on! Out now!' Amber yelled, grabbing him by the arm. 'It's going to explode!'

Alex looked at the jerry cans of fuel wedged under the

bench seats. The big truck was a bomb on wheels. If there was anyone anywhere near the Unimog when it went up, there would be no chance of survival. He jumped out, grabbing a water-filled girba from under the nearest bench as he went. Turning back, he yelled to the others, 'When you get out, run! Follow me and Amber!'

They all scrambled out and began sprinting away from the Unimog, heading for Paulo and the two girls. Amber and Alex were in the lead, Alex carrying the girba slung over his shoulder. Li and Hex took up the rear, with the children in the middle. Li was counting heads as she ran, but she couldn't get the number right. She tried again. There was one missing.

Li slowed, turning a shocked face to Hex. 'Samir!' she gasped.

Hex slowed too, scanning the running children in front of him. Li was right. Samir was not among them. For an instant Hex stood still and a muscle jumped in the angle of his jaw, then he turned round and ran back to the burning Unimog.

'Hex!' called Li behind him. 'Come back! It's too late!'

Hex ran on. As he ran, he muttered over and over to himself, 'What the hell am I doing? What the hell am I doing?' but his legs kept pumping, ignoring whatever his brain thought.

The canvas cover on the back of the truck was alight by the time Hex panted up to the tailgate again. Shielding his face against the heat with his hand, he peered into the smoky interior. At first he thought the back of the Unimog was empty and he had put his life at risk for nothing. Then he saw Samir, still sitting on the bench right at the far end of the truck with his feet not

142

quite reaching the floor and his hair crinkling in the heat. His hands were held neatly together in his lap and his back was straight. He could have been a kid on a school bus, except for the look of frozen terror on his face.

Hex looked up at the blazing canvas roof, then ducked his head and threw himself into the back of the truck. He grabbed Samir by his gandourah and hung on tight as he backed out again on his belly. A piece of blazing canvas fell on to his back and he yelled with pain as the heat began to scorch through to his skin. He fell from the tailgate on to his back with Samir on top of him. He rolled back and forth in the dirt to put out the flames, then he jumped up, hefted Samir under one arm and ran for his life.

Li and the others had stopped a good distance from the Unimog. They watched in horror as Hex disappeared into the smoke surrounding the burning truck. It seemed to take an age before a black silhouette came running out of the smoke again, lit up by the flames behind him.

'He's got him!' yelled Li, spotting Samir wedged under Hex's arm.

'Come on, Hex!' yelled Paulo, urging him on.

Hex was halfway between the Unimog and the waiting group, when the whole thing went up with a massive whump that sent a blast wave of scorching air and flames spreading out from the centre of the explosion. Everyone fell flat and put their hands over their heads as the blast passed over them. Seconds later they were on their feet again, scanning the flame-strewn ground between them and the truck.

'There he is,' cried Alex, pointing to Hex's still form, lying face down on the ground.

They held their breath and watched for one second . . . two; finally Hex raised his head and clambered to his feet. He held out his hand and helped Samir up, then the two of them walked shakily towards the others.

'Since when did you become a hero?' demanded Amber tearfully, giving him a hug.

'Don't know what came over me,' said Hex, grinning down at her. 'It won't happen again, I promise.'

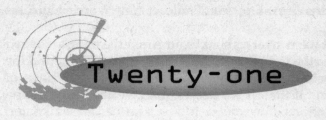

Twenty-one

'Well, the good news is we all survived – and we have some water,' said Alex, patting the girba.

'And the bad news?' asked Amber.

Alex nodded at the shattered shell of the Unimog. Flames and smoke were spouting from it and soaring high into the night sky, well above the top of the rise.

'If the Scorpion is following us, then we've just lit a huge "come-and-get-us" beacon.'

'We should start walking then,' said Amber.

'Where to?' asked Hex, looking around at the dark desert surrounding them.

Amber turned and looked at the sandstone bluff outlined on the horizon. Behind the dark bluff she could see another red glow lighting up the sky. 'Of course!' she grinned. 'Remember that oil installation beyond the bluff? That's the gas flare we can see in the sky. We can head for that. They'll have medics there, and satellite communications – even a helicopter pad.'

'What about the armed guards?' said Alex uneasily.

'They're not going to shoot a bunch of unarmed kids,' said Amber. 'Besides, if the Scorpion is coming after us, I'd rather face them than him any day.'

The bedraggled group moved off through the moon-lit desert, heading for the northern end of the bluff. It took them hours to reach it, and by then Kesia and the

145

younger ones were staggering with exhaustion.

'We have to stop,' said Paulo, casting worried looks at Kesia.

'But we're nearly there,' said Amber, gazing at the red glow in the sky beyond the bluff. 'Once we get round the other side of the bluff, there's only another hour of walking, if that. If we keep going, we can reach the oil installation before dawn. It'll be a far harder walk later, in the sun.'

Kesia moaned and fell to her knees, then lay down on her side and curled up.

'She is my patient,' said Paulo firmly. 'And I say she cannot walk another minute. Jumoke and Samir are out on their feet, too.' He scanned the face of the bluff ahead of them. There were cave openings in the cliff, just as he remembered them. 'We can shelter in one of the caves for a few hours. We will be out of sight, but we can keep a look-out to the north. Once we have rested, then we can finish the walk.'

Amber looked around at the others. They were all nodding, agreeing with Paulo. She sighed as her vision of being whisked off by helicopter to a luxury hotel on the coast faded away. 'OK,' she said reluctantly. 'We find a cave.'

There was one cave at ground level, right on the northern tip of the bluff. They headed for it, with Alex and Paulo supporting Kesia between them, and Hex and Amber giving Samir and Jumoke piggybacks.

'What is that smell?' demanded Amber as they reached the final slope leading to the dark cave mouth.

The group came to a halt. Amber was right. There was a smell coming from the cave that was so strong and acrid, it scraped at the back of their throats and sent them into fits of coughing if they breathed too deep.

'Did something die in there?' asked Hex, covering his nose with his hand.

'No,' said Li, bending in the moonlight to examine a spattering of brown droppings at the cave entrance. 'But there's something living in there.'

She took a couple of steps nearer to the cave and nodded as she saw that the brown spatters thickened inside the cave, covering the floor like a rough carpet. There were thousands of beetles moving busily back and forth across the droppings.

'We can't go in there,' she said, turning back to the others.

'What is it?' asked Paulo.

'Bats,' said Li.

Khalid nodded in agreement. 'Is dangerous smell,' he said.

'Too right it is,' muttered Amber, wiping tears from her smarting eyes.

'It's ammonia,' said Li. 'It's a gas given off by the beetles that eat the bat guano and it's dangerous to breathe it in.'

'OK,' said Alex. 'We'll have to camp outside the cave and hope that overhang up there gives enough shade to hide us if we're still here when the sun comes up.'

They settled down on the rocky ground. Alex handed the girba of water round and Amber produced dates and pistachio nuts from her rucksack. She had bought them in the souk as they were preparing to rescue Li. She forced herself to eat a few dates, even though she was so tired she could hardly chew. The four of them had eaten a hurried meal in the souk earlier, but Amber had to make sure she kept up her blood sugar levels. She pulled her kit from her pouch and tested her blood, then injected herself with insulin.

Paulo tended to Kesia, noting with satisfaction that the only blood on the bandages around her arm was old and brown. The wound had not bled for hours, despite the long walk. He sniffed at the wound, but there was no smell of infection. 'Ask her to wriggle her fingers for me,' said Paulo.

Li translated and Kesia obliged, screwing her face up with pain.

'Good,' said Paulo as he watched her fingers move. 'There is no nerve damage. I think she will be fine once she can get some proper treatment.'

'I'll take the first watch,' said Alex, moving off to sit with his back against a rock that gave him a good view of the desert to the north.

'Wake me after an hour,' yawned Li, checking under the stones for scorpions before curling up in a ball on the ground. The others settled down where they could and soon they were all deep in an exhausted sleep, despite the hard ground. Alex sat on, listening to the gentle snores of the rest of the group and scanning the northern horizon.

Hours later, he opened his eyes with a start. He was surrounded by a fluttering, squeaking black cloud. He sat up, his heart pounding, trying to figure out where he was. The smell of ammonia caught at the back of his throat and made his eyes smart. Alex gasped as he realized that the black cloud above him was made up of hundreds of bats, returning home in the early dawn light. He sat up quickly, glancing around with a shamefaced look as the bats zoomed in low over his head and poured into the mouth of the cave behind him. Not only had he fallen asleep on his watch, he had then slept on until dawn.

Everyone else was still asleep. Alex scrambled to his feet and the stream of squeaking bats parted smoothly around him. He rubbed his stinging eyes, then gazed out into the northern desert. His heart went cold as he saw a small cloud of dust moving slowly across the huge plain that stretched to the northern horizon. It was heading straight for the black streamer of smoke that still rose from the burnt-out Unimog over to the west. Alex groaned. That cloud of dust had to be the Scorpion. He had regrouped, patched up his men and found a new vehicle. Once the slaver reached the Unimog, it would be an easy matter to follow their footprints all the way to the bluff.

Alex gazed at the cloud of dust, estimating that it would take about an hour for the vehicle to reach the bluff. If he got the others moving right now, they might just make it to the oil installation before the Scorpion caught up with them.

The group members were all awake and on their feet in a surprisingly short time. Alex doled out water from the girba while Amber quickly injected her morning dose of insulin. Minutes later they were off, tramping around the northern tip of the bluff and chewing on dates and pistachios as they walked. They moved out of the shadow of the bluff and turned east, into the low sun. The oil installation was spread out on the plain beyond the bluff and they got their first proper look at their destination. One by one, they stumbled to a halt and stared.

'*Dios,*' breathed Paulo, gazing at the thick pall of black

smoke that rose into the sky above the installation and drifted eastward on the wind. Beneath the smoke a huge ball of red and black fire boiled from the ground. The comforting glow on the horizon they had been walking towards all night had not been the gas flare at all. The wells were ablaze and the compound was a shattered ruin.

'What the hell happened here?' whispered Amber.

Khalid spoke up hesitantly. 'I think . . . my friends . . . maybe they do this.'

Alpha Force looked at one another, suddenly remembering the sullen boys in the refugee camp. Amber's uncle must have failed to persuade the news agencies to show the minefield footage Alpha Force had filmed, and the boys had responded with a second, successful attempt to blow up the oil supply pipes.

'But how did they get past all the guards?' asked Amber.

'It's a big space, Amber,' said Alex. 'It's almost impossible to make a whole section of desert totally secure. If someone is determined to get through, they will.'

'Yeah, and those Sahawaris, they're pretty good at sneaking up on you,' said Amber, remembering how Khalid had scared her at the minefield.

'What do we do now?' said Li.

'We have to keep moving,' said Alex, looking over his shoulder. 'I think we should still head over there. There might be people who can help us. A helicopter. Something . . .'

They marched on across the plain as the sun rose higher and the temperature climbed. The closer they got to the installation, the less promising it looked, but they kept going, always keeping upwind of the fires. With the Scorpion on their trail, they had no other option. Finally they reached the high, wire fence that ringed the compound and made their way around to the gates, which were swinging open. Alpha Force stepped inside and looked around for any sign of life. Khalid stood beside them, and Juma and his three followers lined up beside Khalid, wanting to be seen as part of the older group. Sisi helped Kesia to sit down and put a comforting arm around Samir's shoulders, while Jumoke wandered over into the scant shade of the gatehouse, a tiny wooden hut on short stilts. The little girl leaned against the warm wood and drew patterns in the sand with her sandalled foot while she waited for Alpha Force to decide what to do next.

The oil wells burned a good distance away, beyond the back of the compound, but even where they were standing, at the front of the complex, the heat was intense. The air trembled with it. The Nissen-type huts nearest to the wells were charred skeletons. Steel cargo boxes the size of small houses had been lifted in the air by the initial explosion and thrown across the compound. The Nissen huts closer to the front gates were damaged too. All the windows had been blown out by the blast. Doors hung open on their hinges, swinging in the wind. Whole sections of wall had peeled away from one hut, leaving bedrooms and bathrooms open to the sand and wind.

Hex stared in at a small, neat bedroom, with posters and photographs pinned to the wall and a robe hanging from a peg. He was reminded of photographs of bombed houses in his home city of London during the

151

blitz. There was the same sense of something too personal being exposed for everyone to see.

Paulo looked over to the helipad. It was empty. The company helicopter was lying on its side some way off with the rotors twisted and broken. Next to the helipad a short row of black body bags lay in the sand, each with a flapping white label attached to it. Three of the bodies in the bags looked small and slight next to the others and Paulo's stomach turned over as he wondered whether they were the three boys from the camp.

'Hello?' shouted Amber. Her voice drifted on the wind, a faint and tiny noise swallowed up by the vast rumbling of the oil fire. She closed her mouth again, scared at how small she felt.

'I think they've all been evacuated,' said Li. 'The living ones, anyway,' she added, pointing to the body bags. 'They must be coming back for those.'

'Shall we wait here, then?' asked Hex.

'I don't know,' said Alex, glancing over towards the bluff. 'We might run out of time—'

He stopped short as Jumoke gave a high scream. Everyone turned to see the little girl writhing on the ground beside the gatehouse, clutching her foot. Rearing out of the sand above her terrified face, its jaws open wide and its two curved front fangs dripping with venom, was a large, hissing snake.

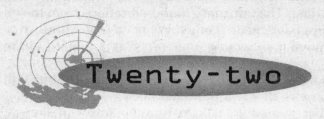

Twenty-two

'Li?' said Alex, without taking his eyes from the snake.

Li had a vast knowledge of plants and animals, learned from a childhood spent on field trips with her parents. Alex had no doubt that she would be able to identify the snake.

'Horned viper,' she said without hesitation, noting the pointed protuberances above the snake's eyes, the thick body and the sandy coloured skin with darker brown markings. She knew this type of snake had a habit of burying itself in the sand, leaving only its eyes exposed and waiting for its prey to pass by. This one had probably been disturbed by Jumoke's foot as she drew patterns in the sand.

'Venomous?' asked Alex.

'Highly,' replied Li.

Alex groaned and took a step towards Jumoke, hoping to pull her out of range. The viper raised its head and rubbed the scales of its back together in a warning rattle.

'Don't move,' ordered Li. 'Everyone! *Ne vous déplacez pas!* They only strike at moving objects.'

'Any chance of it leaving if we stay still?' asked Alex, watching the snake.

Li started to shake her head, then changed her mind as the snake caught the movement and turned its beady eyes on her. 'Normally, I'd say yes, but this one looks pretty riled. The unusual ground vibrations from the oil well fires have made it edgy. We need to get Jumoke to stop moving otherwise that viper is going to strike again.'

'Also, if she lies still, the venom from the first bite will spread more slowly around her body.'

Amber started to talk to Jumoke softly in French, trying to get her to calm down and stay still. Jumoke was too terrified to listen. She continued to thrash back and forth in the sand, clutching her foot. The snake watched her, its wedge-shaped head swinging in time with her movements.

'We have to do something!' whispered Hex. 'That thing is going to bite her again any minute now!'

Slowly, Alex turned his head from side to side, looking for a weapon of some sort. There was nothing but sand all around him. Then he remembered his knife, hanging in a sheath at his belt. It was a single bladed knife with a wooden handle, perfectly balanced and extremely sharp. Alex moved his hand to the sheath and unclipped the top. He slipped the knife from the sheath and slowly, smoothly, went down on one knee.

Alex knew how to throw a knife and this knife was an old friend. With this knife, on a good day, he could throw accurately enough to pin a wasp to a tree.

On a good day.

Alex hefted the knife in his hand and studied the snake's weaving head and the wooden wall of the hut behind it. He would only have one chance. If he missed, he would anger the snake even further and prompt it to bite Jumoke again.

Alex drew a deep, steadying breath and took aim. The

154

knife flew from his hand so fast, no-one saw it leave. They heard the thunk of metal sinking into wood, and suddenly there was the quivering knife handle, pinning the viper to the gatehouse wall. The blade had hit the snake dead centre, just below the head.

Alex stared at the thrashing snake, then down at his trembling hand. Then he suddenly sat down hard in the sand. His mouth had gone completely dry.

Paulo hurried forward and picked Jumoke up, carrying her well out of the way of the snake. They all gathered around him as he laid Jumoke in the sand, making soothing noises as he straightened out her leg and began to examine her foot. He could see beads and trickles of venom on her skin, mixed in with the sand, so he grabbed the girba and unplugged it. He poured water over Jumoke's foot to wash the venom and sand away, then he bent forward to remove her sandal and examine the bite.

'Is it bad?' asked Amber, her voice quavering as she saw Paulo's shoulders begin to shake.

'Very bad,' he said in a strangled voice.

'W-will she die?' quavered Amber.

'No.' Paulo raised his head and Amber saw that he was laughing, not crying. 'But we have a fatally wounded sandal.'

He held up Jumoke's sandal and pointed to the twin gouges in the thick leather straps that crisscrossed over the front. Jumoke stopped crying and stared at her sandal, then at her unmarked foot with such a comical expression of surprise that everyone started laughing.

Seconds later, the laughter died into a shocked silence as a man's voice snapped out an order directly behind them. At the same instant Alex, Hex and Paulo all froze as they felt the cold touch of steel on the nape of their necks. Alex tried to stand but the rifle muzzle jabbed into his neck, forcing him down. The man's voice snapped again, speaking in Arabic.

'He say to kneel,' said Khalid, in a trembling voice. 'Kneel slow and put hands so.' Khalid demonstrated by putting both hands on the top of his head, then he repeated the order in French to make sure everyone in the group understood.

Paulo and Alex were already down in the sand. Slowly, Hex knelt beside them with the cold rifle muzzle never leaving the back of his neck. Carefully he raised his hands to his head as Li and Amber kneeled down on either side of him, their eyes big with fear. The children all followed their lead, apart from Jumoke, who remained sprawled in the sand, too frightened to move.

Once everyone was down on their knees, the man who had barked the orders moved round to stand in front of them, with two of his men. Alex saw that all three were carrying high-powered semi-automatic rifles. With the three rifles that were still digging into the backs of their necks, that made six weapons, and his only weapon was stuck in the wall of the gatehouse. The rifle muzzle against his head made it hard to think straight, but Alex forced himself to stay calm and assess the danger.

The rifles the men were carrying were old AK-47s, with a wooden breech and handle, but Alex could see they had been well cared for. Besides, AK-47s might be ugly looking, but they lasted well and could withstand a lot of dirt and neglect. They were designed for fast, close-quarter combat, being short and easy to handle. The magazine carried thirty rounds and the pistol grip meant that they could be fired from the hip, or even one-handed in the hands of an expert – and Alex could see that these men were experts by the way they handled their weapons. Alex abandoned any hope of fighting his way out of this one.

Hex also studied the three men in front of him. Even though he was sweating with fear, his photographic memory seemed to be working on automatic pilot and was insisting on feeding him all sorts of stored information from the research he had done before they came out to the Sahara. The men were all wearing a sort of combined turban and veil in a dark blue material. That was a sure sign that they were Tuareg, members of a race of nomads who pre-dated the Arab civilization in the Sahara. They were a war-like people, who had never managed to repel the invading Arabs and Turks or, later, the French, because they were too busy feuding amongst themselves. Looking at the fierce, dark eyes that glared out at him from the swathes of indigo material, Hex could see that these men would think nothing of killing him. He felt a cold snail-trail of sweat slip down his back.

The leader of the Tuareg glared at them all for a few seconds, then he squatted down in the sand and lifted Jumoke to her feet. He turned her gently this way and that, checking her for injuries, and Amber suddenly understood what he was thinking.

'Oh!' she gasped. 'They think we were torturing Jumoke! Imagine how it must've looked to them – her screaming on the ground and us all huddled around her. Khalid, quickly, explain to them what really happened.'

Khalid nodded, then let fly a stream of Arabic, gesturing to Jumoke and the pinioned snake on the gatehouse wall as he spoke. Slowly, the men's eyes became less fierce as they listened to Khalid and then bent to inspect the still-twitching viper. Finally the leader lowered his veil, revealing a thin, lined, hook-nosed face, and his men followed suit. He looked at Alex and said something in Arabic.

'He say, good aim,' translated Khalid.

Alex nodded and smiled tentatively at the men. They might have dropped their veils, which he took as a good sign, but their AK-47s were still trained on the kneeling group.

The leader gave more orders in Arabic. Three of his men peeled off, running towards the Nissen huts. They were carrying large hessian sacks. The other two stepped forward and, talking casually to one another, began to search the group.

'What's going on?' demanded Li, as the watch and opal ring she had only recently claimed back from Amber were expertly removed.

'They're here to loot,' said Hex grimly, as his own watch disappeared into the robes of one of the men. He nodded over at the three who were going through the abandoned Nissen huts, taking anything of value. 'There's a long tradition of banditry amongst some Tuareg tribes.'

Paulo gasped. 'These men are bandits?'

'Looks like it,' said Hex.

'But aren't they going to help us?' asked Li as the two men finished relieving them of their valuables and headed off to join the others in the Nissen huts.

Hex nodded over at the six camels, tethered by their nose rings to the chain-link fence. 'I think that once they've taken what they want, they'll be out of here.'

158

'But they can't just leave us here!' said Amber.

Alex looked up at the leader, who was now lounging against the gatehouse wall, watching them idly. Would he leave them here if he knew about the Scorpion? The man had reacted with anger when he thought they were hurting Jumoke. Perhaps, if he knew their story, he would help. There was only one way to find out.

Alex turned to Khalid. 'Khalid, can you tell him who is after us?'

Again Khalid launched into a long stream of Arabic with many hand gestures, pointing north past the bluff, then south in the direction of Samir's village. He pointed to Samir as he explained what had happened to Hakim, then he gently touched Kesia's arm, showing the man the bandages. He turned Li's face for the man to see the cane slash across her cheek and lifted his sirwal to show the weals on the backs of his legs. Finally he came to a stop and sat back down on the sand. The man looked them over impassively.

'Look over there,' said Paulo, pointing over to the bluff.

A vehicle had just cleared the northern tip and was heading towards the oil installation in a cloud of dust. It would reach the compound in about fifteen minutes. 'It is the Scorpion,' said Paulo. 'We have just run out of time.'

Khalid started speaking again, pleading with the man. Amber joined in, speaking in French. The leader sliced both hands through the air in a silencing gesture. Slowly he turned to look at the approaching vehicle, then he shrugged, turned away from the group and called for his men. They gathered their haul together, strolled over to the camels and tied the sacks to the sides

159

of the wooden saddles. Once the sacks were secure, the men untethered the camels and looked over at their leader, waiting for the command to move out. The leader began to walk away from the group of children and Alex slumped, feeling the hope drain out of him.

Then Jumoke stood up and hurried after the man. She came up alongside him and slipped her hand into his. *'S'il vous plaît?'* she said softly. 'Please?'

The nomad stopped and looked down at the little girl and Alex held his breath.

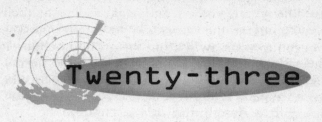

Twenty-three

The Scorpion's lip curled in a sneer as he peered through the windscreen of his brand-new Land Rover at the approaching line of camels. Tuareg. Scavengers and bandits. They had been stripping the deserted oil installation. He could see all sorts of stuff hanging from their saddles. There was even a small fridge strapped to the back of the biggest beast.

The men walked alongside the camels, their faces hidden behind their blue turbans and veils. The women rode high on the beasts' backs in ones and twos, wrapped from head to foot in bright swathes of cloth. The Scorpion glimpsed a group of blue-turbaned children scampering along on the far side of the camels, half hidden by the big beasts. A flicker of interest briefly crossed his face. If he could not find his missing stock of slaves, he would need to find replacements for his buyers. But even if he could persuade a Tuareg to part with his children, they would never make good stock. They were too fierce and independent.

The Scorpion turned away, dismissing the children. Instead he brought the Land Rover to a stop next to the man he judged to be the leader of the group and pressed a button to wind down the window. Instantly, hot, dry air flooded into the car, destroying the air-conditioned comfort within. The Scorpion grimaced with annoyance.

When he found his escaped stock, they were going to suffer for this.

The leader and two of his men halted by the car and stared in impassively while the camels moved on by with their slow, swaying walk. The three men were armed with AK-47s, but then so were his men, so he was not too concerned. Without much hope, the Scorpion launched into a description of the children he was looking for, but to his surprise the leader nodded. Yes, he had seen those children. The Scorpion sat up. Where were they now?

The Tuareg pointed back towards the oil installation, then up at the sky. An evacuation helicopter had flown in and taken them all away. The Scorpion snarled and slammed his hand against the steering wheel. He closed the window, put the Land Rover into gear and drove on to check it out for himself. Behind him, the Tuareg walked on through the desert without looking back.

It was not until they reached the Tuareg camp that the leader allowed Alpha Force to unwrap themselves from the brightly coloured sheets they had stripped from the beds in the compound. The Tuareg shouted at the camels and pulled their nose rings until the big beasts went down on to their bellies, rocking violently back and forth as they folded first their front, then their back legs. Alex, Amber, Li, Paulo and Hex slid gratefully to the ground and gazed around the camp, their faces hot and sticky from their time under the sheets. Kesia, Khalid and Sisi slid down to join them.

Beside them, Samir, Jumoke, Juma and his gang unravelled their blue turbans, which were made from torn sections of a roller towel, taken from a bathroom back at the compound. They all grinned at one another. The disguises had worked. They were safe. For now.

The leader of the Tuareg came up to Alpha Force and solemnly handed back their watches and jewellery.

'Please, tell him to keep them,' said Amber to Khalid. 'We can never pay him back enough for saving us.'

Khalid shook his head. 'He say, you are guests now. He do not take from guests. He say his camp is yours.'

They thanked the leader, who bowed his head gravely, then went off with his men to unload the camels. A Tuareg woman hurried over with a jug of water and a brass dipper. She held the jug while they each took a dipperful of water and drank thirstily. Their throats were dry, their lips cracked by the hot desert wind and the water was cool and soothing. The woman smiled and hurried off again and Alpha Force and the children were left to wander around the camp.

The Tuareg tents were low, oval structures pitched in the lee of a small rise, which shielded the camp from the worst of the desert wind and also hid it from any passing travellers. Containers of water and goat's milk were propped in the shade of the tents, while thin strips of meat were set out on racks to dry in the sun. Next to the drying racks was the main cooking fire for the camp, where a group of Tuareg women were already busy preparing a goat and couscous stew for their guests.

Amber and Hex wandered over to the fire, followed by Kesia and Sisi. The fire was fuelled with dried camel dung and it seemed to need a lot of puffing and blowing to get it going. Hex went down on his hands and knees and blew until the fire was crackling and he was red in the face. The Tuareg women giggled behind their hands at the green-eyed youth who was prepared to help with the cooking. Hex grinned back at them and settled down next to Amber with his eyes watering from the smoke.

'Watch it,' muttered Amber, more than a little jealous. 'If you make yourself too useful, they might want to keep you.'

Jumoke, Samir and Juma's gang went off to make friends with a gaggle of Tuareg children, while Li, Paulo and Alex strolled over to watch the camels being unloaded. Li was fascinated by the big beasts. They crouched in the sand while the men unloaded them, contentedly chewing on the dried fodder their owners had laid out for them and batting their long curved eyelashes to keep the drifting sand out of their eyes. They were all different. One big beast with a coat that was nearly white swung its neck like a snake, trying to take bad-tempered bites out of its neighbours, while a little camel with a deep red coat watched with a mild, long-suffering expression on his long face as the other camels stole most of his share of the fodder.

Once the saddles and saddle cloths were removed, they were revealed to be single-humped camels, or dromedaries. The humps wobbled from side to side as the men urged the beasts to their feet again. The men bent to hobble their front legs with rope, before removing the head ropes that were threaded through the nose rings. The camels wandered off to the edges of the camp to forage for food with the rest of the herd.

The men motioned to Li, Paulo and Alex to follow them over to the largest tent in the camp. A faded carpet had been spread on the sand in the shade of the tent and two large, shallow communal bowls of goat and couscous had been placed in the middle of it.

'We helped cook it,' said Amber proudly, passing around big flat ovals of freshly baked bread.

Somehow, the six Tuareg, the five members of Alpha Force, Khalid and all the other children managed to squeeze around the two bowls of food. Alex watched the men carefully. They held the bread between their fingers and used it as a plate, pushing the food on to it with their thumbs.

'You must only use right hand,' warned Khalid. 'Left hand is forbidden.'

Alex nodded, then reached forward and pushed the hot food on to his bread and took a bite. The goat meat had a strong, gamey taste and the couscous was soft and buttery. It tasted wonderful.

After the meal came the ceremony of the tea. The Tuareg men sat back and lit little brass pipes while the leader sat cross-legged and placed a brass tray in front of him. The tray was loaded with glasses into which he put chunks of sugar, hacked from a solid cone with his knife. He then poured green tea into the glasses from a great height, so that the sugar dissolved and the tea frothed up to the rim. The glasses were handed round, drained, then handed back for the next person to use. The tea was sweet and strong and they all had three glasses before the leader of the Tuareg finally sat back and began to talk to Khalid.

Khalid listened, nodded, then turned to Alpha Force. 'He say, he do not think this man will give up. He wonders, what you do now?'

They looked at one another.

'We can't stay here,' said Amber reluctantly. 'He's right, the Scorpion isn't going to stop looking for us and we don't want to put these people in any more danger.'

Alex nodded in agreement. 'So where do we go?'

'We take Samir back to his village,' said Paulo simply. 'That is what we promised to do.'

'And then we wait,' said Li darkly.

'For what?' asked Hex.

'For the Scorpion,' said Li. 'He'll turn up at the village sooner or later, to see if Samir has returned home. When he does, we'll be ready for him.'

Khalid explained their plan to the Tuareg leader. He listened, asked a few questions, then spoke again.

'He say he know the village of Samir,' translated Khalid. 'For now, we sleep. Tonight, he and his men will take us there.'

It was a strange, dreamlike trip they took through the desert that night. The Tuareg had woken them from an exhausted sleep at dusk and given them a meal of bread, dates and tea. Six camels were already loaded and saddled, with head ropes threaded through their nose rings.

While the Tuareg men waited, Amber sleepily administered her insulin injection and Paulo changed Kesia's bandages, noting with satisfaction that the wound was still clean and free from infection. Once they were ready, the Tuareg men led the camels out of the camp, slipping between the low dunes in their indigo robes like moving pieces of twilight.

The Tuareg's gliding walk was deceptive. They set a hard pace as they tramped steadily across the desert, eating up the miles. Samir and Jumoke sat together on one camel and Kesia rode a second. The journey developed a gentle rhythm as the camels swayed along on their broad, two-toed feet. Alpha Force and the other children shared the remaining four beasts between them, turn and turn about, sometimes walking and

166

sometimes riding. The moon rose, a million silver stars speckled the dark sky and they moved on in silence, wrapped in their own thoughts.

They only halted twice. The first stop was at the little cairn of stones behind the rise, halfway between the village and the sandstone bluff. Paulo and the Tuareg leader climbed the rise, carrying a length of clean, plain cloth and some thin rope. The other men stood sentinel to the north and south of the rise with their rifles slung across their shoulders. Alex, Amber and Paulo held the head ropes of the camels while Li took Samir and the other children a little way off and sat with them, her arm resting lightly around Samir's shoulders.

When Paulo and the Tuareg leader descended the rise ten minutes later, they were carrying Hakim's body, wrapped in the length of clean cloth and secured with the rope. Paulo's expression reflected a mixture of sadness and peace of mind as he helped to settle Hakim in a specially constructed cradle strung from one side of the little red camel. He was saddened all over again at Hakim's death, but it felt right to be fulfilling his promise to bring both brothers home.

The second stop was much further on. Two hours before dawn the Tuareg called a halt on the banks of a wadi. The men passed around a girba of water and the leader showed Alex how to dig a deep hole on the outside bend of the wadi. As Alex watched, the hole in the dry river bed gradually filled with water. It was poor stuff, brown and brackish, but the camels drank it readily enough and Alex made a mental note to remember that trick if he was ever unlucky enough to be stranded in the desert without water.

They reached Samir's village just after dawn. Their

camel train had been spotted a long way off, and by the time they approached the straggle of mud-brick houses a hostile group was waiting for them on the edge of the village, armed with rifles.

'What's going on?' demanded Amber. 'Why do those men have guns?'

Khalid explained that there was no love lost between Arab villagers and Tuareg nomads. The name had been given by the Arabs and it meant 'abandoned by God'. The Tuareg preferred to call themselves *Kel Tageulmous in Tamachek*, a mouthful which translated as 'people of the veil'.

'But why don't they like each other?' persisted Amber, eyeing the rifles of the village men as the camels swayed steadily nearer.

'The Tuareg – this is their land, long time back. They think, Arab not belonging here. The Arab, they have many times the Tuareg raiding their villages.' Khalid shrugged. 'Is how it goes,' he finished.

The tension increased as the camels drew closer to the village. The Tuareg did not help matters by veiling themselves so that only their eyes showed like black stones through a slit in the cloth.

'After all this, there'd better not be any shooting,' muttered Hex, watching the village men's fingers straying closer to the triggers of their rifles.

Suddenly Samir spotted his father amongst the crowd. With a cry, he slid recklessly from the saddle while his camel was still moving. The Tuareg leading the beast reacted quickly and managed to catch Samir before he hit the ground. He set the sobbing boy gently on his feet and they all watched as Samir ran towards his father and jumped into his arms.

The village men did not know how to react. Some lowered their guns; others raised them to their shoulders. The Tuareg tensed and swung their AK-47s from their backs.

'Khalid!' hissed Amber. 'Explain. Fast!'

Khalid stepped forward and began to talk to the village men. Alex realized that he could pretty much guess what point Khalid had reached in the story by watching the changing expressions on the faces around him. They went through a whole range of emotions from disbelief, to anger and, finally, to sorrow.

When Khalid had finished, Paulo and the leader of the Tuareg lifted Hakim's body down from the little red camel and carried him over to his father. The gaunt-faced man set Samir on his feet and held out his arms for his other son. They laid the wrapped body gently in his arms and he cradled the boy for a moment, his face full of grief.

Finally he raised his head, looked the Tuareg leader in the eye and spoke to him. The Tuareg inclined his head, then took hold of his camel's head rope and began to lead the beast over to the village well at the centre of the tired little plantation of date palms. The other Tuareg followed, each inclining his head gravely to Samir's father as he passed.

'What did he say to them, Khalid?' asked Alex.

'He say the best thing to a Tuareg,' whispered Khalid, his eyes damp with tears in his scarred face. 'He say, like brother, "our water is yours".'

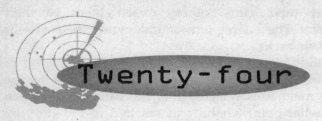

Twenty-four

The Tuareg left an hour later, with their camels watered and their girbas full. Alpha Force watched from the outskirts of the village as the swaying camels and the men in blue robes walked off into the rising heat of the day, but the Tuareg never once looked back.

They buried Hakim in the dusty little graveyard on the edge of the village later that morning. The whole village was there, standing out in the merciless heat of the sun to say their farewells. The women wailed and wept over the grave. Hakim's mother was inconsolable and had to be supported by two other women as the burial went on. Samir stood on the opposite side of the little grave, dry-eyed now, with his father's hand resting on his shoulder.

Alpha Force, Khalid and the other children kept to the back of the crowd, feeling awkward and out of place. Li decided she would come back to the grave later, when everything was quiet, to say her own goodbyes.

After the burial there was a village meeting. Alpha Force had already warned the people that they thought the Scorpion would come searching for Samir. Lookouts were posted around the edges of the village and the rest of the people gathered in a shady courtyard at the heart of their community to decide what to do next.

The meeting was held in French, the only language common to everyone there, although Alex, Hex and Paulo found it a struggle to keep up with what was being said.

'When the Scorpion arrives, we will kill him and his men,' said Hakim's father and the village men cheered, shaking their rifles in the air.

Amber looked at the others and they nodded at her to go on. She was the best French speaker and they had made her their spokesperson. She rose to her feet and waited for the people to grow quiet before she spoke.

'My friends and I think that would be wrong,' she said. 'If we kill these men, then all the people who have helped them to sell children into slavery will go free. If we capture the Scorpion and hand him over to the proper authorities, then the whole trafficking ring will be caught.'

'The authorities have done nothing to stop him so far,' called a voice from the back and the people shouted in agreement.

'I promise you they will do something this time,' said Amber stoutly. 'There are international agencies who have been after this man for years. If they have the Scorpion, they will make sure the rest of the trafficking ring is destroyed. My uncle is a powerful man. He will also make sure of this.'

The people murmured unhappily. They had just buried one of their own and they wanted their revenge. Amber could see that she was losing them, but she kept trying.

'If you kill these men now, their organization will continue. More children will die. Children like Hakim.'

The discontented murmuring grew in volume and a

few men raised their guns in the air again. Amber felt her heart sink. Then Hakim's mother stood up and gazed around the small crowd. With her face drawn with grief and her eyes red from weeping, she made a powerful figure, and the people grew quiet to hear what she had to say.

'Our oldest grandfathers still remember a time when great trade caravans of camels passed through here, carrying salt, spices, ostrich feathers, gold and copper. Our village was a good place to live then. The wells were full and the caravans brought us wealth.' She paused, looking around as the people nodded in agreement.

'But now our village is dying. The drought has sucked dry all the wells except one and the caravans have stopped passing through. Instead, big trucks carry the trade goods along black roads far to the east of our village.'

Hakim's mother paused again and looked across at her husband. The next thing she had to say would be difficult for both of them. 'That is why we let the Scorpion take Hakim and Samir away with him. We thought we were doing the best for our sons.' She searched for Samir and her dark eyes softened as they lingered on him for a moment, but when she faced the villagers again, her eyes were hard. 'That man promised us he was taking our sons to a better life. He promised us they would be taught a trade and find work in Morocco. So we let them go. This morning we had to bury one of them. I do not want any more children to die. I want to catch *all* the slavers. I say we listen to the American girl!'

This time the murmurings were in agreement. Amber relaxed as Hakim's mother sat down again. The tide was beginning to turn.

'How will we capture them?' asked a young man. 'You tell us they have Kalashnikovs. We have rifles but nothing to match those weapons.'

'We shall not use guns,' said Hakim's mother, rising to her feet again. 'When the Scorpion comes, we shall hide Samir and his new friends away. Then we will welcome these men back to our village with a special feast.' She held up her hand to stop the outraged shouts of the crowd. 'This feast will have one very special ingredient. Dried henbane leaves.'

Li smiled and nodded her approval of the plan. She knew all about henbane. It was a narcotic plant and the leaves were the most powerful part. Dried, powdered henbane leaves were readily available in all the souks of the Sahara. They were used in small quantities as a painkiller and a sedative, but in larger quantities the plant was a deadly poison.

'What is this henbane?' asked Paulo. 'And what will it do to the Scorpion and his men?'

'It'll turn them all into sleeping beauties,' grinned Li. 'As long as the village women get the dosage right, the Scorpion and his men will fall into a deep sleep, almost like a coma. It could last for days.'

'When they are asleep,' said Hakim's father, 'we shall tie them up and hold them prisoner until the proper agencies arrive.'

'But how shall we bring the agencies here?' asked one of the men.

The villagers fell silent. Theirs was a poor village. There was no radio mast or satellite dish here for them to communicate with the outside world.

'I can answer that,' said Hex, standing up. 'The Scorpion is driving a new Land Rover. I had a good look at it from under my sheet as the Tuareg smuggled us past. I saw a satellite phone clipped to the dashboard. Once the Scorpion is asleep, we can use his phone to arrange for his arrest!'

The villagers roared with laughter at the idea of using the Scorpion's own phone to make the call that would finish him, and the meeting broke up on a high note. The men went off to relieve the look-outs and to prepare a room that would be strong enough to hold the prisoners in case they woke up before the police arrived. The women clustered together to plan the feast.

All afternoon they worked, using food stores they could ill afford to lose and burning fuel that was in short supply. Alpha Force were very tired after their night of walking but they were determined to help. While Khalid and the other children slept, Li and Amber chopped and stirred with the village women and Alex, Hex and Paulo took their turns on watch. All five of them hoped they were right about the Scorpion. If he did not follow them back to the village, all the planning and work would have been for nothing. They could still report him to the right people, but the Scorpion had a knack for disappearing whenever the authorities thought they were close to catching him. If the Scorpion did not come to the village, there was no guarantee that he would ever be caught.

By the end of the afternoon all the food was ready. There was a rich bean soup, spiced chicken with orange peel and olives, a tagine of lamb with prunes and almonds, and a dish of sweet rice with raisins and cinnamon. It looked and smelled wonderful.

Amber stared at the little piles of dried, crushed henbane leaves, which were set out ready to add to the

174

dishes at the last minute. 'How do you know the right dosage?' she asked the women.

Samir's mother eyed the piles of grey powder. 'The trick is to add enough to put them to sleep but without making the food taste bad. I think that is about right.'

'And you're sure it won't kill them?' asked Li.

Samir's mother shrugged as though she did not really care. 'If one man eats like a pig, then he might not wake up again. But as long as the other two live, we can still find out about the rest of their contacts.'

She looked at Amber and Li with a grim smile, then looked again, noticing their tired faces. 'Now,' she said. 'All we can do is wait for our guests to arrive. And we can do that without your help. Go back to my house and sleep. We will wake you if anything happens.'

Li and Amber were too tired to argue. As they stumbled through the darkening alleyways to Samir's house, they were joined by an equally tired Paulo, Hex and Alex. In the main room of the house they rolled out the sleeping mats that had been left for them and lay down side by side. Five minutes later they were all deeply asleep.

It was Khalid who woke them a few hours later. He started with Hex, who was nearest to the door.

'Go 'way,' snapped Hex irritably, turning over on his mat.

Khalid moved on to Alex, crouching over him in the dark room and shaking him by the shoulder. 'What?' muttered Alex. 'What is it?'

'Headlights,' hissed Khalid. 'We see headlights, in the desert. They are heading for the village.'

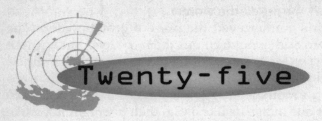

Twenty-five

'It is them,' whispered Paulo, raising his head to get a closer look at the approaching vehicle. 'It is their Land Rover.'

'Get down!' hissed Alex, digging his elbow into Paulo's ribs. 'If they see us up here, everything'll be ruined.'

Alpha Force were all lying on the roof of a house on the northernmost edge of the village. All the village houses had flat roofs which could be reached via a set of stone steps built on to the side of the house; each roof had a low, whitewashed wall around the edge. Paulo ducked his head back down behind this low wall and flattened himself on to the roof as the Land Rover rumbled past beneath them, heading for the village square.

Once the Land Rover had turned into the next street, Alex clambered to his feet and the other four joined him. They stared across the moonlit rooftops. The route to the main square was marked out for them. On every rooftop that bordered the way, one or two village men in dark robes were in position, their rifles trained on the street below in case anything went wrong.

'Let's go,' whispered Alex.

Alpha Force turned and ran for the edge of the roof. They stepped up on to the low wall and launched themselves into space, soaring across the narrow alleyway below. They landed on the next rooftop and continued running with hardly a break in their stride. All along the route the Land Rover was taking, the village men were doing the same. As soon as the vehicle was past them, they picked up their rifles and followed it, jumping from rooftop to rooftop like large, black bats.

By the time the Land Rover came to a stop in the main square, Alpha Force and the village men were in place on the surrounding rooftops. Samir, Jumoke and the others were hidden away in a village house well away from the square, with a reluctant Khalid to watch over them and keep them quiet. Now everything depended on the village women and the remaining men putting on a good act.

The plan was that they would come out to greet the Scorpion and his men, looking pleased and surprised to see them again. Samir's mother would ask after her sons. Li's guess was that the Scorpion would be brazen and tell the villagers that Samir had run away before he could be apprenticed. Samir's mother would be outraged at this slur on her family honour – money had changed hands and her son had then broken the agreement. She would invite the Scorpion and his men to stay as their guests while they waited for her wayward son to return.

Alpha Force watched from the rooftop as the Scorpion and his men clambered from the dusty Land Rover. The traffickers were wary as they scanned the quiet square and they held their Kalashnikovs at the ready in case of a hostile reception. When the village men and women emerged from their houses, all calling and holding out their arms in greeting, the Scorpion relaxed. A slow smile spread across his face and he signalled discreetly to his men to shoulder their weapons.

'It's working!' whispered Amber, watching the pantomime below.

Samir's mother stepped straight up to the Scorpion, asking after her sons. The Scorpion began to talk, and as she listened, the eager expression on her face was replaced with outrage. She shook her head and put her hands on her hips as he told her about Samir's ungrateful behaviour, then she and her neighbours took the Scorpion and his men by the arms and led them into the shady courtyard off the main square where, eight hours earlier, the whole village had planned their ambush.

Alpha Force moved across to the rooftop of one of the houses edging the courtyard, moving fast and silently and keeping low. They watched as the villagers brought out a carpet and cushions and settled the Scorpion and his men. The men sat cross-legged on the cushions and propped their weapons beside them. Of the three of them, only the Scorpion looked uncomfortable. His tight western jeans were not made for sitting cross-legged on cushions and he kept tugging at his waistband.

First the women brought water for the three men to wash the dust from their hands and faces. Then came glasses of green tea; finally the steaming bowls of food were brought out and placed in the middle of the carpet.

'That's it,' muttered Hex, his green eyes glinting as he watched the men take their first bites of the food. 'Eat up, boys.'

The men were hungry and the food was good. The two henchmen set to, stuffing it into their mouths and swilling it down with glasses of water. The Scorpion ate much more slowly, stopping often to ease his waistband away from his belly.

'Will he eat enough?' asked Amber anxiously.

'We'll soon see,' whispered Alex.

It did not take long. Twenty minutes later the two henchmen were sprawled on the cushions with their heads resting together, snoring heavily. The Scorpion was propped up against the wall of the house behind him with his head back and his mouth open. Slowly, Alpha Force and the men on the rooftops clambered to their feet and looked down. In the courtyard below the actors stopped their charade, and for a few seconds everyone was still, staring at the three unconscious men. Then Hakim's mother produced a coil of thin rope from within her robes and held it in the air. Quickly, three other village women stepped up to help her. They moved the two Kalashnikovs out of the way, propping them up against the house wall next to the Scorpion, then they flipped the first henchman over on to his belly and yanked his hands behind his back. The rest of the women began to clear away the contaminated food.

Up on the roof, Alpha Force stood in a circle and grinned at one another.

'We did it!' laughed Amber.

'*They* did it,' corrected Hex, nodding down to the women in the courtyard.

Amber made a face at Hex. 'Whatever. I'm gonna call my uncle and get him to send the cavalry in. You coming?' She turned on her heel and headed for the steps that led down to the Land Rover in the main square.

Hex sighed and looked at the others. 'What can you

do with her?' he said, shaking his head before he followed Amber.

Alex and Paulo headed the other way, leaping across the moonlit rooftops towards the house where Khalid and the children waited. Paulo wanted to be the first to tell Samir the good news. Li stood alone on the rooftop for a moment, hesitating. Her head was full of thoughts of Hakim and she was not sure she wanted to be in the middle of a crowd of excited children. She chose the quieter option and followed Amber and Hex towards the Land Rover.

Down in the courtyard the women finished trussing up the first henchman and moved on to the second, bending over their work. Behind them the Scorpion twitched, then his mouth snapped shut and his eyes fluttered open. He turned his head and stared blearily at the women for a few seconds, then his eyes sharpened as he realized what they were doing. Reaching out, he grasped one of the Kalashnikovs propped against the wall next to him and, using it as a crutch, he levered himself to his feet. The drug was making his brain slow and stupid, but he knew one thing. He had to get away. He turned and walked out of the courtyard with exaggeratedly careful steps, heading for his Land Rover.

Li stepped out into the main square, following Amber and Hex. She stopped when she saw that quite a crowd of villagers had gathered around the Land Rover to listen to Amber make her call. Li watched them for a moment. Everyone else seemed to be celebrating their success, but now it was all over she could only feel a deep sadness. It was as though she could only now start mourning for the brave young boy who had died trying to save his brother. Li looked down a moonlit side street.

At the end of the street, the desert opened out. Hakim's grave was out there in the dusty little graveyard. Li remembered her promise to go back to the grave later and say her goodbyes. Now would be a perfect time. She could let Hakim know that his brother was safe and his killers were caught.

Li turned away from the square, then stopped as she heard a retching noise in the street behind her. Someone was bending over and vomiting his stomach contents into the dust. Li stepped forward to see whether she could help, and the Scorpion straightened up and looked straight at her.

He recognized her instantly. His eyes and his brain were a lot sharper now that he had rid his system of the henbane-laced food. His face was hard and he only staggered a little as he moved towards her, raising the Kalashnikov to his shoulder. Li wasted two precious seconds while her shocked brain adjusted to this new threat, then she moved into a fighting stance, judging distances. She tensed, preparing to leap high in the air and knock the weapon from the Scorpion's hands. It was a risky move but she was counting on the henbane he had digested slowing his reactions enough for her to reach him before he could fire the gun.

Just then, she heard the laughing voices and running feet of Khalid, Jumoke and the other children. They were coming closer, heading for the main square to join in the celebrations, and Li knew they were going to appear round the corner any second now. She hesitated. Suddenly the stakes had changed. If her leap failed she was putting all their lives at risk as well as her own. Li looked down the quiet alleyway leading out to the desert and made a split-second decision. Instead of leaping towards the Scorpion she dived down the side street, leading him away from the children.

Li flew down the alleyway. As she ran, her headcloth fell off and her long black hair streamed out in the moonlight. She heard running footsteps behind her. The Scorpion was following. Li felt her back muscles clench as she imagined a few rounds from a Kalashnikov slamming into her spine. She found more speed in her legs as she pushed on towards the end of the alleyway and burst out into the open spaces of the desert.

Li sidestepped and pressed herself against the wall of the last village house as she looked frantically around the flat desert, trying to think of a plan. She had to lure the Scorpion away from the village and then try to take his weapon from him. She shuddered to think of the damage he could do in the crowded main square with a semi-automatic Kalashnikov. Her frantic gaze skittered over the little graveyard, then stopped on the oasis.

She headed for the grove of stunted date palms. If she could get the Scorpion in amongst the trees, she would be able to surprise him, she was almost sure of it. One good kick to the side of the head would finish what the henbane had started. As Li sprinted away across the desert, the Scorpion stumbled out of the end of the alleyway. He raised the gun to his shoulder and found her in his sights. The barrel of the Kalashnikov wove from side to side as he tried to focus and the back of Li's head kept appearing and disappearing in the cross hairs.

With a curse, the Scorpion threw the gun to one side and headed off after Li, pulling his wickedly curved knife from its sheath as he ran. That was all he needed to kill this troublesome girl. He could finish her quickly and quietly, without attracting the unwelcome attention the noise of the Kalashnikov would bring, then he could make his escape.

The Kalashnikov clattered when it hit the stony desert floor. Li glanced back over her shoulder and saw the Scorpion jogging towards her. The knife in his hand glinted in the moonlight. Li smiled. Now he had been stupid enough to throw away the gun, all she had to do was hide until she had the chance to slip away. She could leave him stumbling about in the desert, while she headed back to the village to warn the others, picking up the Kalashnikov on the way.

Li reached the oasis and darted in amongst the trunks of the date palms, slipping between them like a shadow. Her confidence faltered as she saw that, close to, the trees were thin and sparse. The double trunks were too slender even for her to hide behind and the ground beneath the trees was flat and open. She glanced back and saw that the Scorpion was closing in. She looked up, thinking about climbing one of the date palms, but the feathery tops would provide little cover, and if the Scorpion spotted her, she would be trapped up there.

Li turned, desperate to find somewhere to hide. Her gaze swept past the village well, then stopped and returned to it thoughtfully.

When the Scorpion staggered into the oasis less than a minute later, it was quiet and empty. He frowned and turned in a slow circle, peering between the slender tree trunks, then he did the same again, this time looking at their feathery tops. There was no-one there. The Scorpion walked over to the concrete wall surrounding the well. He put one foot on the wall and peered down into the well. It was a deep well and the moonlight only illuminated it part of the way down. The rest was in darkness.

The Scorpion straightened, then spotted the bucket made out of a tyre inner tube. The bucket was tied to a long coil of rope, which was itself attached to a rusting metal ring set into the circular concrete wall. The Scorpion sneered at the makeshift bucket. He could not quite believe that this scrawny little village had tried to take him captive. When he had made his escape, he would come back here with reinforcements and make them regret what they had done. He lifted the pathetic inner tube contraption and flung it down the well.

Li was hiding deep inside the well. She had climbed down without a rope, using a free-climbing technique. Pressing her back against one side and her feet against the other, she had used her legs and elbows to move slowly down into the depths of the well. The shaft was lined with palm trunks and the spaces between the trunks had been filled with a mixture of clay and palm fibre. The surface was ideal for chimney climbing, with plenty of nooks and crannies for her to wedge her feet into. She sat comfortably, below the reach of the moon's faint light, staring up at the pale circle at the top of the well and waiting for the Scorpion to go looking somewhere else.

When the bucket came tumbling down the well towards her, Li nearly fell. Quickly, she jammed her elbows into the walls, wincing as the rough surface grated the skin from her arms, then she spread her feet far apart for balance and jinked her body to one side. The bucket caught her hip as it passed and she bit her lip to stop herself crying out with the pain. The bucket careered on down the well shaft and splashed into the murky water at the bottom. Seconds later, it shot past her again, as the Scorpion hauled it up by the rope. Water showered over her, making the walls of the shaft slippery and harder to grip. Li cursed under her breath and held on.

The Scorpion let the bucket drop a few more times, then hauled it back up to the top of the well and dumped it on the wall. He turned and walked off, kicking stones out of his way as he went.

Li listened as the Scorpion's footsteps died away. She waited for a few more moments, but the oasis above her was silent. Her arms and legs were aching from holding herself in position and she dared not wait too long in case the Scorpion was heading back into the village. She shook the water out of her eyes and began to chimney-climb back to the top of the shaft.

When she reached the top, Li cautiously raised her head above the concrete wall and looked around. The oasis was quiet and empty. She scanned the surrounding desert, then looked towards the village. The Scorpion was nowhere in sight but she could see his Kalashnikov, still lying on the ground beside the last village house and glinting in the moonlight.

Li nodded with satisfaction, then gripped the concrete lip of the well with her strong fingers and levered herself on to the wall, preparing to head back to the village and warn the others. As she straightened up on the edge of the well shaft, a dark shape rose from behind the low concrete wall and something slammed into her stomach.

Li gasped and doubled over at the sudden, burning pain in her belly. She turned her head and looked straight into the grinning face of the Scorpion. He twisted the knife in the wound and she cried out and fell to her knees. She felt the knife being yanked out again and she cupped her hand to her stomach. When she pulled it away again it was covered in her blood, shining like black tar in the moonlight.

Li tried to call for help, but her lungs didn't seem to work properly and only a whimper came out. Her head was wrenched back as the Scorpion grabbed a fistful of her hair and pulled hard, exposing her neck. She kneeled on the concrete lip of the well, clutching at her belly as the Scorpion stroked his bloodstained knife across the pale curve of her neck, preparing to slit her throat.

Li could feel herself starting to pass out. A red mist was coming down over her eyes. She marshalled the last of her strength, stiffened her arm and sent it catapulting back against the Scorpion's legs. It caught him squarely across the knees as he stood on the concrete wall beside her. The knife flew from his hand and he staggered backwards. The heels of his cowboy boots slipped over the edge of the well shaft and he windmilled his arms, trying to regain his balance. For an instant it seemed as though he would make it, but the remains of the henbane in his system made his legs fail him at the last second. He fell back into the well, grabbing at Li's long black hair as he went.

Li felt a huge pain in her head and her whole body jerked back, following the Scorpion down the well. Then the clump of hair the Scorpion was holding came out at the roots and she sprawled on the wall with the top half of her body inside the shaft. The Scorpion fell without a cry but she could hear his bones cracking as he hit the walls on the way down.

'That's for Hakim,' she whispered as she heard the body hit the bottom of the shaft with a dull thud and a splash of water. She hung balanced over the well and a red mist filled her head, then turned to deepest black.

Twenty-six

There was a bright light.

Li swatted at the light with her hand but it wouldn't go away.

'Li. Wake up.'

Someone was pinching her earlobe with sharp little nips. Li frowned in annoyance and heard Paulo laugh softly beside her.

She opened her eyes and squinted up into his face. 'Will you stop that?' she tried to say, but all that came out was a moan.

'Hello,' said Paulo, smiling down at her.

'Where am I?' asked Li.

'Oh, that's an original line,' drawled Hex from the other side of her. Li turned to him in annoyance and wished she hadn't. She closed her eyes until her head stopped spinning.

'You're in a private hospital in Rabat,' said Alex, his face swimming into view above her.

'Rabat?' asked Li faintly.

'Its the capital of Morocco, dummy,' said Amber, appearing beside Alex.

Li scowled again. Here she was, lying in a hospital bed after defeating the Scorpion single-handed and all they could do was insult her.

The Scorpion!

Li's eyes widened suddenly and she tried to sit up. An iron band of pain around her belly made her sink back into the bed again. 'The Scorpion,' she whispered. 'In the well.'

'Not any more,' said Alex. 'He's lying in a morgue.'

'And his men and his mother are under arrest and telling lots of tales,' added Amber.

Li gave a satisfied smile. She had vowed to get the Scorpion and his mother and she had succeeded. Her hand reached down, exploring her belly. There was a surprisingly small dressing on the left side of her stomach, which hardly seemed to account for the amount of pain she was in. 'What happened?' she asked.

'Another original line,' drawled Hex. 'They just keep coming.'

'Shut up, Hex,' said Paulo mildly.

'But I'm allowed to tease her, now she's out of danger,' said Hex.

'I was in danger?' asked Li.

'The knife sliced through your intestines,' explained Alex. 'And there was a lot of internal bleeding. By the time Amber's uncle arrived with the helicopters, you were in a bit of a state.'

'That is an understatement,' said Paulo, his face becoming serious for a minute as he remembered how they had nearly lost Li.

When Hakim's mother had come running into the main square to warn them that the Scorpion had escaped with one of the Kalashnikovs, they had wasted valuable time searching the village before they had discovered Li, lying still and pale beside the well in a spreading pool of her own blood.

'Helicopters,' said Li, and a vague memory came back

to her of three black shapes cutting across the desert sky with their searchlights trawling the ground below. She remembered the blatting of the rotors and Paulo shielding her with his body from the blast of sand as the helicopters landed.

'You were airlifted here and went straight into surgery,' said Alex. 'That was two days ago.'

'Two days!' gasped Li. 'How did I lose two days?'

'Drugs,' said Hex briefly. 'Lots of drugs.'

'Sedatives and painkillers,' explained Alex.

'And am I OK now?'

'Why don't we let the surgeon tell you that?' said Paulo. He moved back and Philippe Larousse took his place, smiling down at her.

'Philippe!' she cried, then winced as a stabbing pain shot through her.

'That will get better soon,' said Philippe. 'I repaired your intestine and stitched you up. You've been on intravenous, high-dosage antibiotics to prevent peritonitis.'

'That's when your belly fills up with all the icky stuff from your punctured intestines and gets infected,' explained Amber with relish.

'The antibiotics should counteract any infection,' said Philippe, giving Amber a look. 'You're going to be left with a scar in your side, but otherwise you should make a complete recovery.'

'Thank you,' said Li, reaching out to squeeze the French surgeon's hand. She licked her lips thirstily. 'Can I have some water?'

They raised her bed slightly and poured out a beaker of iced water. Paulo held it to her mouth and Li sipped carefully. As she sipped, she spotted a familiar scarred face grinning at her from the bottom of the bed.

'Khalid!'

'He would not leave,' said Philippe. 'Not until he knew you were recovering.'

Khalid moved up to the side of the bed. 'I have news,' he said. 'Amber, her uncle, he give me a—' He stopped and looked over to Amber for help.

'A grant,' said Amber.

'Yes! A grant. I am to go to school, then when I old enough, I train to be a doctor. I go back to help in the camps, just like Dr Philippe!'

'That's wonderful, Khalid,' smiled Li. 'You'll really make a difference.'

'Is a better way, I think, than the path my friends take. They all die for nothing.'

'So it *was* your friends at the oil installation?' asked Li.

Khalid nodded.

'I'm sorry,' whispered Li, remembering the three small body bags in the oil workers' compound. 'I wish our minefield footage had been shown. It might just have stopped them.'

'Oh, it was shown,' said Hex, with a touch of bitterness. 'But only after the attack on the oil installation. The attack was the big news, not the Sahawari camps or the minefields. It seems we value oil more than people.'

'What about Jumoke and the others?' asked Li. 'Where are they?'

Amber took over. 'That's where my uncle is now. He's gone with the aid agencies to return them to their home villages. Philippe made sure Kesia's arm was sorted before she went. The aid agencies are going to see what they can do in the villages, with my uncle's help. No-one should be so poor they have to sell their children in the hope of giving them a better life. Oh, and Jumoke left this for you.'

Amber laid a square of sugar paper on the bed. Li looked down at it and her eyes filled with tears. Jumoke had drawn a picture of herself standing between her mother and father. All three of them were smiling broadly, and a bright yellow sun shone overhead. Underneath the picture Jumoke had written, 'Beloved One'.

'We did good,' whispered Li, looking round at the others.

'We did good,' agreed the rest of Alpha Force.

'Excuse me?' said Khalid. 'We – did – good?' He raised his one eyebrow disapprovingly. 'That is not correct English.'

The four of them looked at Khalid, then turned and looked questioningly at Li.

'Bed bath,' she ordered.

Minutes later, the two young Moroccan women at the nurses' station jumped as a series of high screams came from the room at the end of the corridor. They both dropped their charts and began to run towards the closed door, but it suddenly burst open and a young Arab boy with a badly scarred face came running out. He was soaking wet and clutching his shirt to his chest. His eyes were bright with laughter as he skidded past the nurses, followed in quick succession by five people waving dripping flannels. There was a fair-haired boy, a tall black girl, a South American boy who winked at them as he ran past, a green-eyed boy and, finally, the respected French surgeon who had arrived at the hospital by helicopter two days earlier.

The horrified nurses watched them disappear round the corner at the other end of the corridor, then hurried into the room to check on their patient. Li was lying in the bed, clutching her side and gasping. Tears were running down her face.

'Do you have some pains?' asked one of the nurses, leaning over her.

'No,' gasped Li, trying to stop laughing. 'They all just left.'

CHRIS RYAN'S TOP TEN TIPS FOR SURVIVAL IN IN A DESERT

● ●

Near the beginning of this story, Alex gets the rest of the Alpha Force team to recite back to him the basic rules of any survival situation – shelter, water, food and fire – and these four factors certainly are vital for survival in a desert. However, if travelling into a desert anywhere in the world, you really do need to know a little more if you are to survive the merciless heat of some of the hottest areas in the world. Temperatures can rise to over 120 degrees Fahrenheit in the summer months!

1. Planning

First off, never ever set out into a desert region without others knowing your travel plans, how long you plan to be away and the exact route you are aiming to take. Desert regions can be vast (the Sahara covers thousands of square miles!) and it will help in any rescue attempt if you stick to your plans as much as possible.

Equipment is also vital. When the Alpha Force team set out in the Unimog, they take sand ladders, shovels, spare fuel, plenty of water, communication equipment etc, and Alex is never without his basic survival kit. Members

of the SAS are trained in survival techniques, yet if setting
out on foot into a hot, dry area like a desert, each man
would probably carry something like up to 100 lbs (or
45 kg) of equipment – and that would be mostly water and
supplies to ensure survival.

2. Water

This is absolutely VITAL to your survival – you've all seen
the movies of people staggering around in deserts dying of
thirst and the heat of the environment will make you lose
fluids quickly as heat makes you sweat (sweating is a way
of the body trying to cool itself down). Without water, you
could only last about two and a half days maximum in a hot
desert – and that's if you stay in the shade and don't move!
On the move, in full sun, without water, you'd be lucky to
get as far as seven kilometres before you start passing out.

Fluid loss will produce a range of symptoms, from thirst,
flushed skin, sleepiness and feeling sick to dizziness, a
headache and an inability to walk – even a swollen
tongue if it gets serious. At the first signs, stop, rest and
drink some water. Once I walked until I collapsed, I had
really bad dreams, hallucinations and felt really sick.

Make sure you carry sufficient water with you on any
desert expedition, and plan your route to pass by oases,
wells and waterholes (these will be marked on maps).
Remember, though, that wells may be deep and there might
not be a handy bucket available; take a container and some
rope with you so you can refill at wells wherever possible.
If you are in a group, and you don't know when rescue

might be coming, ration your water to be on the safe side.

The Tuareg also showed Alpha Force a handy hint too: there could be water available at the lowest point between dunes and you can dig for this, just like they did. Make sure, though, that you wait until it's dark; if you try digging in full sun, you'll lose precious fluid through sweating.

To keep fluid-loss down to a minimum:
- Find shade. Get out of the sun. If possible, don't lie directly on hot sand – try to raise yourself up from its surface so that air circulates all around you.
- Don't waste energy – and fluids – by moving about. Try to rest whenever you can.
- Save your breath – talk as little as possible, and breathe through your nose, not your mouth.
- Eat only if essential; food requires water to be digested.

If a shortage of water is likely to be a problem, you can collect as much as a litre over a 24-hour-period if you make a solar still to collect evaporated water at night. Dig a hole about half a metre deep and about a metre across, then lay a sheet of plastic loosely across it, dipping in the centre to make the water run to a point. Then simply place a container under this point to collect the water.

3. Shelter

Shade – and shelter – is really important to protect you from the sun. Just like the creatures that live in the desert, you need to learn to make the most of any available shade

– shadows from the walls of wadis, or rock outcrops, for instance. You could also use the nighttime to collect rocks and build a small shelter as a windbreak, draping clothing over it during the day to provide some protection from the sun.

If you're in a broken-down vehicle, and you have told people where you are going and for how long, you should stay with the vehicle, making it easier for rescuers to find you, and providing shelter for you during the day. Don't stay inside it, though – metal containers get really hot in desert sun; it's better to use its shade or rig up a shelter alongside it.

4. Clothing

Learn from the locals – the people who live in and travel through the desert. Wear flowing shirts and baggy trousers to increase air circulation and help prevent excessive sweating. Keep it loose.

Headgear is also important to protect your head and neck from the sun's rays. Again, copy the desert peoples and fashion protection from any piece of cloth, draped over your head so that it hangs loosely down over your neck. You can wrap it round your face for warmth at night, or pull it across your face if caught in a sandstorm.

You should also protect your eyes from the glare of the sun. Your equipment should include sunglasses or goggles made specially for desert conditions. If you don't have these, protect your eyes from any sand blown around in the wind by covering them with cloth, cutting small eyeholes to enable you to see.

It's also amazing how painful it can be to walk with sand in your boots, so wrap cloth round your boots to try and keep out the sand. And a final tip: if you do take your boots off, make sure you shake them well before you put them back on again – you could find a scorpion or small snake has decided your boot will make a nice new home! I once found a snake in my sleeping bag; it was a cold night and the snake had crawled in there to keep warm. They curl up and go quite docile. I got out of my sleeping bag and shook it out!

5. Fire

In such hot conditions, fire might be the last thing on your mind, but the temperature can drop very rapidly overnight during winter months and a fire will provide much-needed warmth. Most desert scrub is very dry and will burn easily and, if you are following trails used by others, you might well find camel droppings too, which make great fuel.

You can use the fire to boil water for hot drinks, food (crumble a stock cube into hot water for an instant pick-me-up) or for treating any injuries. Its smoke will also be useful if there are rescuers out looking for you.

If you find yourself without matches, use the power of the sun's rays focused through a piece of broken glass or a magnifying glass, camera lens or similar to form a pinpoint of light on your unlit fire. If you keep it steady, the fire should catch alight (you might need to blow on it gently once you get a glow).

6. Food

It's time for a diet, I'm afraid, if you're stuck in a desert. Food may be one of the four survival essentials, but you can actually live for about three weeks without food, and as food requires water for digestion, it's best to eat as little as possible. Fortunately, you probably won't feel very hungry!

If in a group, ration out supplies to the barest minimum, eating anything perishable first as it will spoil very quickly in these conditions. Avoid eating foods that are fatty, however, as fats take a lot of fluid to digest.

When I was escaping through the desert in the Gulf War, I had no food and that wasn't really a problem, because I didn't miss it. Your stomach shrinks so you don't feel any hunger.

7. Navigation

In the middle of a desert, every dune can look the same and it is possible to convince yourself you are walking in a straight line and then find you have walked a circle. What a waste of energy! Some basic navigation skills can really help save your life if you have to be on the move.

Firstly, check out the position of the sun. In the *northern* hemisphere, when the sun is at its highest point in the sky, it will be due *south*. In the *southern* hemisphere, at midday, it will be due *north*. A stick about a metre long will help you find north too, at any time of the day the sun is in the sky. Find a patch of clear ground and stand the stick upright in the ground. Mark where the end of its shadow falls – use a pebble – then wait at least fifteen minutes and mark the new position. If you join these two points, this will be an east-west line and north-south will be at right angles to this. Remember, the sun rises in the *east*, and sets in the *west*, so you should now know which direction is which. You can do this at regular intervals if you are moving to make sure you are keeping going in the direction you want.

Secondly, it's worth learning – before you go anywhere dangerous – how to recognize some of the major stars in the sky. In the northern hemisphere, the Pole Star is exactly due north and in the southern hemisphere, a constellation called the Southern Cross can be used to find south. Why not check out some books on the skies from your local library and try identifying the stars? It's a useful skill that could, one day, save your life.

Finally, as you travel through an unknown terrain, you can mark specific points by using little piles of stones or similar – like Khalid does – and by making notes of what you pass. If you have to leave a group to find help, making a map like this would mean you could find your way back to them. Always have an emergency R.V. (rendezvous) to find your way back to. Whatever method you use, you must keep it simple because, when you are tired and hungry, it is hard to concentrate. Again, this is something you could practise at home – even in a local park.

8. Weather

You may think it is always just hot and sunny in the desert, but this isn't quite true. There can be sudden dust or sandstorms or, in some deserts, flash floods which are produced by sudden torrential rain. If you get stuck in a sandstorm, sand will enter virtually every possible orifice in your body (ouch!) but the most important parts to protect will be your eyes and nose so that you can keep on breathing. Wrap cloth around your head and aim to take shelter immediately. It's a good idea to pack a shovel or two with your equipment; a sandstorm can produce a lot of sand in a very short period of time and you might need to dig yourself or someone else out – or dig your vehicle tyres out of soft sand when driving in dunes. When I have been in the desert, I have seen vehicles buried under sand so it is very important to keep all your equipment together so if you are hit by a storm, you don't lose anything.

9. Illness and injuries

Even the smallest scratch can easily get irritated by sand or infected if not treated immediately. Alex carries potassium permanganate in his survival kit as this creates an antiseptic if added to water, and I would certainly recommend to anyone going into a desert environment to make sure they carry some kind of antiseptic to treat any wounds. You might also pick up a thorn and these must be pulled out immediately (even if they're in an embarrassing place, so watch out where you sit down!).

Sprained ankles or ligaments are also possible if walking through – or climbing up – deep sand. Don't try to set a faster pace if travelling than the weakest person can manage and, if you do sprain an ankle, yet have to carry on walking, keep your boot on or the ankle might swell and you won't be able to get your boot on again.

Finally, do keep an eye out for insects or snakes. Most of them would much prefer to leave you alone, but you do need to be aware that the desert is home to quite a few creatures you would rather not get to know – and many of them will be using the same places to take shelter that you pick. Scorpions, for example, may shelter under rocks. Watch where you step, shake out any clothing or bedding material – and your boots – before you use it and don't panic if you do come face-to-face with a snake. Try not to move suddenly (many snakes attack movement) and just back off very slowly.

10. Signal for rescue

If you planned your expedition properly, there should almost certainly be people out looking for you quite soon after you become lost or stuck. This can take time, however, and it's worth being prepared to make their job as easy as possible by using signals. A couple of signals that could be used are:

Fire: smoke makes a good signal, so have a fire ready and make sure you can light it promptly.

ROCKS could be arranged in the sand to spell out the universal call for help: SOS.

In daytime, use the **sun's rays** to attract attention by angling a piece of glass, or even a bit of shiny foil, to catch the rays and flashing a light. Remember: if you repeat any signal three times, with pauses between, this is the international signal used by someone requiring help.

If you had established a camp when you first became lost, and then had to move for some reason, leave clear direction signals at the original campsite so that rescuers will know where to look eg: if you plan to walk north, arrange stones in the sand to form an arrow in that direction with a large N by it.

BE SAFE!

Chris Ryan